THE NIGHT CALLING

RITE WORLD: NIGHT WOLVES BOOK 1

JULIANA HAYGERT

COPYRIGHT

This book is a work of fiction. Names, characters, places, and incidents either are products of the author's imagination or are used fictitiously. Any resemblance to actual persons, living or dead, events, or locales is entirely coincidental.

Copyright © 2022 by Juliana Haygert

All rights reserved. This book or any portion thereof may not be reproduced or used in any manner whatsoever without the express written permission of the publisher except for the use of brief quotations in a book review.

Manufactured in the United States of America.

First Edition May 2022

www.JulianaHaygert.com

Edited by H. Danielle Crabtree

Proofread by Jessica Nelson

Cover design by Claire Holt with Luminescence Covers

Any trademark, service marks, product names, or names featured are the property of their respective owners, and are used only for reference. There is no implied endorsement if one of these terms is used.

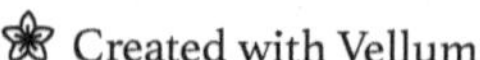 Created with Vellum

AUTHOR'S NOTE

I hope you enjoy reading *The Night Calling*!

This book is set in a bigger "universe", called Rite World, where many of my series take place. This "universe" is still our modern world, but with a large, hidden supernatural society. Because there are many series in this same universe, there will be many cameos in my books, but don't worry. Book 1 of any new series is designed to be a good entry point into this universe. Hopefully, you'll like it a lot and will pick up the other books too! <3

RITE WORLD

Welcome to the RITE WORLD!

For a printable reading order, type this link on your browser: http://www.julianahaygert.com/wp-content/uploads/2022/05/Rite-World-Reading-Order.pdf!

Free Novellas:
The Vampire Hunt
The Light Witch

Novellas:
The Hunter Path
The Light Calling
The Light Witch
The Wicked Alliance
The Shadow Fae

Rite World:
The Vampire Heir (Book 1)
The Witch Queen (Book 2)
The Immortal Vow (Book 3)
The Warlock Lord (Book 4)
The Wolf Consort (Book 5)
The Crystal Rose (Book 6)
The Wolf Forsaken (Book 7)
The Fae Bound (Book 8)
The Blood Pact (Book 9)

Rite World: Blackthorn Hunters Academy
The Demons Kiss (Book 1)
The Hunter Secret (Book 2)
The Soul Bond (Book 3)
The Shadow Trials (Book 4)
The Immortal Vow (Book 5)

Rite World: Vampire Wars
The Darkest Vampire (Book 1)
The Darkest Witch (Book 2)
The Darkest Magic (Book 3)

Rite World: Night Wolves
The Night Calling (Book 1)
The Night Burning (Book 2)
The Night Hunting (Book 3)
The Night Rising (Book 4)

Rite World: Lightgrove Witches
The Midnight Test (Book 1)

The Midnight Spell (Book 2)
The Midnight Flame (Book 3)

And more to come!

THE VAMPIRE HUNT

I have an exclusive novella set in the Rite World that is just for my newsletter subscribers!

Go to https://www.subscribepage.com/JuHNLFB to sign up and receive your book!

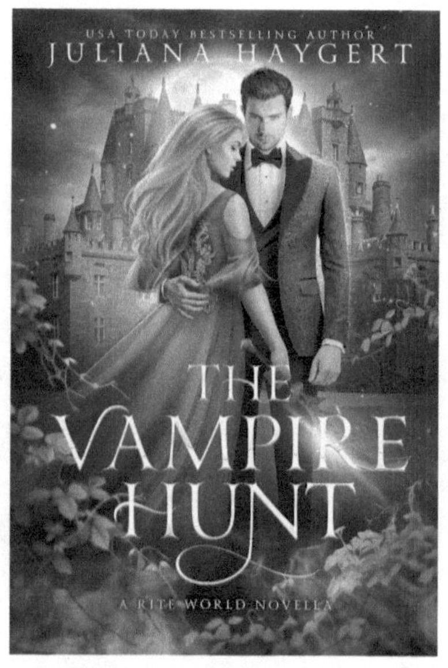

THE VAMPIRE HUNT
A Rite World Novella

Norah is a demon hunter, one of the best graduated from the Blackthorn Hunters Academy. When she's sent to investigate a case concerning demons in a small town, she runs into a very arrogant vampire. Her first instinct is to kill him, after all, he's a supernatural and demon hunters are taught to end all evil.

Cain is a vampire prince. Because of his status, he's in charge of making sure humans don't find out about his kind. During a routine investigation, he bumps into a very sexy demon hunter and he wonders what she's doing on his way.

However, the case grows much bigger for Norah and Cain to handle alone. To find the truth and win this battle, the vampire and the demon hunter will have to hunt together—without killing each other.

How well could this end?

1

RAIKA

I LIVED IN A GILDED PRISON.

There were fleeting moments, a few seconds here and there, when I forgot. And all I had to do to be reminded of my prison was glance over my shoulder. A demon was always a few feet back, watching me.

Making sure I didn't try to escape.

Again.

I sighed and rinsed my mug in the sink, my eyes across the marble counter, where Minsi was seated finishing her cereal.

For her, I tried my best to make this house—her house—not look like a prison, despite a second demon in the corner of the room watching her. Worse than these two was the other half-wolf, half-demon who lived in this house as if he were the king.

Well, in a way he was. Conri was the damn alpha, and we could do nothing about it.

I glanced across the family room to the left, where the foyer was located. Around a corner was the home office.

Conri was in there and I knew that because of the two demons stationed outside the door.

Demons infested this gilded prison.

A door opened. I dropped the mug in the sink and went to Minsi. I pulled her chair back and helped her stand.

"Why don't you go upstairs and finish getting ready?"

She pointed to her unfinished cereal.

I grabbed the bowl and handed it to her. "You can finish it in your bedroom."

Heavy footsteps echoed through the house.

"Just ... go."

Her hazel eyes widened, understanding dawning on her. With trembling hands, she took the bowl from me. The metal shackle on her wrist clinked mine, but we pretended we didn't hear it or feel it. I had decorated mine with leather straps and metal spikes and Minsi's with pink yarn and bedazzle. Better to pretend these were pretty bracelets than shackles.

I clenched my teeth, watching as the ten-year-old girl disappeared from the kitchen as if it was on fire, going for the second set of stairs in the mudroom, the demon Dixon following her.

Heavy footsteps grew closer, and knowing I couldn't avoid the devil, I turned toward him.

A wide smile spread across his lips as he entered the kitchen—the two demons stayed back.

To me, Conri looked like an MMA fighter with his cropped dark hair, trimmed beard, and stocky body. He wasn't the tallest wolf, but he was muscular. He wasn't one bit attractive and yet he had an imposing air around him, as if everything about him, even his movements, yelled he was the supreme predator here.

"Good morning, Raika," he said, his deep voice with its usual chipper tone. It made me sick.

I crossed my arms. "What do you want?"

Conri gave me a once-over, as usual. I wanted to duck behind the island or run and hide in a hole every time he did that, but I wouldn't give him the satisfaction of knowing he bothered me.

I did my best not to squirm as he took in my appearance. I had been dressing in the same style for years now—cropped tank, shorts, fishnet tights, long boots, and sometimes a leather jacket if the weather called for it. All black, of course.

"Come talk to me," he finally said, settling his eyes on mine. He gestured behind him.

This mansion didn't look like a prison with its wide spaces and fancy country decorations. There was a formal living room, a family room, an entertainment room, a dining room, a breakfast room, and a sunroom with another long table to seat ten, two kitchens—one inside, another outside on the porch—and eight suites on the second and third floors with en suite bathrooms. The few times I had seen this house when I had been a child, a pang of jealousy had cut through me. The chic, white contemporary farmhouse style with medium wood accents had always been my favorite, and now I lived in it.

I hated it with all my body and soul.

"I'm good here."

Used to my retorts, Conri's smile didn't lessen. "Suit yourself."

He walked into the high-ceiling family room and hovered before the large stone fireplace. Two leather armchairs faced the fireplace, and Conri could often be found seated in one of them, drinking whiskey.

This time, though, he didn't sit down. He stood there, his back to the fireplace. "For a while now, my gang and I have been gathering during the full moon to celebrate, and I think it's time we did something bigger."

Despite myself, I walked to the edge of the kitchen, where I could hear him better. Of course, the demon who watched me, Phell, moved with me.

"What do you mean?" I asked.

"In less than two weeks, it'll be my anniversary as the pack's alpha, and I thought it would be a good idea to have a celebration in the main square with the entire pack."

I blinked. Holy shit, was he insane? Yes, yes, he was. "No one in the pack will want to celebrate that with you. There's nothing to celebrate." In fact, if we did something on that date, it would be to mourn everything we lost—our loved ones and our freedom.

His smile faded. "I'm giving them an opportunity. If they want to be in *my* pack—"

"They don't want to be *your* pack." Conri stilled, his eyes rounded, and a vein on his neck popped. I crossed my arms and lifted my chin. "I don't either, for that matter. I'm here because you force me to be."

Conri's eyes turned yellow and he advanced two steps. My insides tightened, but I held my ground. Hell would freeze over before I showed him fear.

"You will convince them to—"

"I don't think you heard me," I cut him off again. I was treading in dangerous waters. I knew it was stupid, but some-times I couldn't help it. I loathed this wolf-demon with all I had, and since there was no one else to talk to, to scream at, he served the bill. "The pack won't come to your event, no

matter what you want me to tell them. And I won't come eit—
"

Conri's hand closed around my throat, yanking me upward. My toes barely touched the ground and I struggled to breathe. He leaned into me and bared his sharp, canine teeth in my face.

"You don't get to choose," he snarled. "You will do as I tell you, little wolf, or you know what will happen." He dropped his hand and retreated a step. I gasped for air, my knees wobbling for having to bear my weight again so suddenly.

I slipped my hand inside my shorts pocket and gripped the long, metal nails I had there. It would be so easy to slip them in and swipe at his face. To hurt him.

But I had done that before, more than once actually, and all I got was a slap so hard that I went careening across the room. Minsi also suffered—he had left her locked in her bedroom for two days without food.

The bastard.

I let out a long, steadying breath.

As much as I wanted to beat him, certain battles weren't worth the fight.

"Oh," Conri started, his voice back to normal. "Next week is Minsi's birthday, isn't it? One year since everything changed. We should celebrate that too, even if only the three of us. Please, dress her up in something nice and—"

I lost it. I slipped two of the metal nails into my fingertips and swiped at him.

Conri didn't seem startled as he stepped back, avoiding my swing by half an inch. A second later, the two demons were on me, holding me back.

Conri smiled at me, but this time, it was a predator's grin. "You naughty little wolf. When will you learn there's nothing you can do? You lost. Your mother is gone. Your friends are gone. Your weak alpha is gone. There's no escape from this, and the sooner you accept it, the better."

Still worked up, I jerked against the demons' hold. Why me? Why did he single me out? Lucille was prettier and nastier. She would have fit his style much more. But ... this wasn't romantic, or for desire. Conri had never attempted to kiss me, to sleep with me. But since the attack, since he took over and became the alpha, he had ordered his demons to keep me safe while he slaughtered everyone else. Then he brought me to live with him at the alpha's house, but never explained why.

"You know I'll never behave," I gritted out.

With a snarl, Conri let his hand fly. My head snapped to the side with the strike, pain spreading through my cheek and jaw.

"The next one will be on Minsi," he barked. "Take her out of my sight!"

The demons holding me dragged me back and into Phell's hand. He grabbed my wrist and forcefully pulled me back into the kitchen and toward the mudroom. I watched Conri as he turned his back on me and walked back to the fireplace, muttering things not even my wolf ears could hear.

I could have fought, but I didn't because I knew Conri would hurt Minsi ... and I would never let that happen.

2

RAIKA

I PUSHED THOUGHTS OF CONRI OUT OF MY MIND AS I JERKED out of Phell's grip and disappeared into my room, shoving the door closed behind me. I rested my back against the solid wood, taking a deep breath to calm my racing heart. When the adrenaline subsided, I finished getting ready for the day because I wouldn't let the devil ruin my day so early in the morning.

Phell and Dixon stood guard from the ends of the hallway —they never came inside our bedrooms. I stopped at Minsi's bedroom and knocked on the door. When she didn't answer, I opened it and spied inside.

Minsi's bedroom was fit for a princess: a white twin bed with four posters and pink gossamer, a white dresser and silver-framed mirror with swirls and details, a large desk piled with books, a swinging chair in a corner, and a huge dollhouse. She had a walk-in closet in addition to the en suite bathroom.

Minsi was the youngest child of Franc and Petra, the previous alpha and his mate, and she had been adored and cared for like a porcelain doll. Her bedroom, her pink and princess-like clothing, her expensive toys reflected that. But they had never helped her make friends. That was the reason she had turned to books when she was younger.

I smiled at seeing her lounging on her bed, legs crossed, and a thick book in her hands.

"Ready to go?" I asked her.

As if just realizing I was there, Minsi lifted her eyes from the book. She nodded, dropping the book onto the comforter.

Without a word, she grabbed her backpack from the desk and walked out of her bedroom.

Ignoring Phell and Dixon as they followed us, Minsi and I descended the back stairs and exited the house through the mudroom door. Minsi didn't question it, because she probably knew we were going the long way to avoid running into Conri.

We reached the long stone path that cut through the front lawn and led us to the main road, from where we could see the rest of the town in the distance. This house, the alpha's house, was located at the southern edge of town. We could have taken a car, but the weather was so nice today—it was May and despite us being in northern Canada, we lived in our own bubble—I wanted to enjoy the warm sun and smell the flowers lining the stone sidewalks.

The Nightshade pack was nestled in two valleys deep into Canada's frozen landscape, but magic kept the pack lands warm and green as if it was always spring. The town had been designed in a perfect grid with the main square at the center where pack events were held. Shops and restaurants and other services surrounded it, and houses branched out from there. Everything was in the same farmhouse style with white or beige or soft yellow walls, several shades of brown for roofs and porches with swings or rocking chairs.

Around the main square were also the town tall, the infirmary, the school, and the library.

On the other side of the main square was the burnt part of town. I always tried to keep Minsi away from there. She didn't need to see that.

I stopped with her at the library's entrance.

"I'll be back later, okay?" I said the same thing every day, and Minsi only nodded. "You'll know where I'll be if you need me."

Again, she nodded and went in and locked the door from the inside. Dixon stayed by the entrance. This was the one sacred place for Minsi and me, and no damn demon or wolf who followed Conri was allowed inside. I had fought Conri for it, and since I had amused him, he relented.

I entered the building across the main square—the school—and Phell didn't stop at the entrance. I could do nothing to keep the demons away. In fact, this was the place with the greatest number of demons in town. In the entire pack lands.

I walked past two demon patrols in the wide corridors and headed to the kitchen. The demons stared at me, snickers stamping their faces—their human faces. These bastards wore human flesh, but I knew these weren't their true form.

I called them demons in my head even though I knew most of them weren't just demons. Most were half-demons, half-wolf shifters like Conri. Somehow, they had found each other and banded together.

I didn't consider them true shifters, though, not like the rest of the pack. Our wolf and our human forms made up two halves of a whole. As for the demons, I didn't want to know about what they were made of.

Rue was already in the kitchen, cutting vegetables with a sharp knife. Two demons stood at the other two entrances, watching her closely.

A small smile adorned my lips as I approached her. Rue was one of the oldest wolf shifters in the pack, and despite wolves being known for their short temper, she was kind and calm. In all the years I had known her (twenty years, aka all of my life.), I had never seen or heard her lose her cool.

She was also my favorite person in the pack, aside from Minsi.

"Raika, dear." Rue handed me the knife and the chopping board. "You're early," she said, her voice thin and frail.

"So are you." I took over the vegetable cutting duties while she went to the stove and checked the pots and pans. "What are you making today?"

"Something simple." She added some of the chopped potatoes to the big pot with boiling water. "A creamy chicken soup and some homemade bread." She opened the oven and checked on the big loaf of bread in there.

There was nothing simple about her cooking. Anything Rue made turned out delicious. I was glad she was the one helping me with these tasks.

I glanced at her over my shoulder. At almost two hundred years old, Rue was agile and energetic for her age, but sometimes I saw her catching her breath, or putting a hand over her heart, when she thought I wasn't looking.

Before everything changed, Rue had been my English teacher from the time I was a pup to the day I graduated at seventeen. She had been the only kind face in school, the only one who considered me another wolf in the pack, and not a cockroach.

She was the reason I loved books so much. When I was about eight years old, the other wolves in our class decided it was let's-make-Raika's-day-hell. She didn't allow it, but she also couldn't stop a dozen wolves by herself, so she took me to her office in the school, which was filled with books. She told me to stay in there for a few hours and relax. She would be back later to take me home. At first, I barely moved, afraid of messing up her office, but it didn't take long for my eyes to turn to the books and skim the spines. I picked one, to pass the time, and by the time Rue returned, I had read almost half of the book. She let me take it home. Later that week, she came up with a field trip for the class: the library. It had been my first time stepping in there, and it felt like entering heaven. I went back almost every day of my life ever since.

I returned my attention to the chopping board. "How are they this morning?"

Rue clicked her tongue. "Same as every day. Half just lie there waiting for time to pass, while the other half are agitated. Tyren rammed against the door a couple of times earlier."

I shook my head. Rebelling like that and acting stupidly would only make things worse. But we had been at this for almost a year now. Would things ever get better?

I doubted it.

Rue and I finished lunch, served several portions in small paper bowls, and placed them on a cart. We also had a big water bottle and a stack of small paper cups to pass around.

Once we had everything, I pushed the cart out of the kitchen and into the corridor that led to the classrooms. Because the school only served our community, it wasn't large. We never had more than one or two classes per grade, ten to twenty kids in each class, and usually had the same teachers in every grade. We learned most of what was taught in the human world, but we also had special subjects like *Wolf 101*, or *Living in a Shifter Community*, and *Honor and Loyalty*.

That was all ancient history now.

Two demons stood by the new wall and door installed in the middle of the corridor. They saw Rue and me approaching and unlocked the door, opened it, and let us pass. Once we were through, they closed and locked the door again.

The moment we stepped into this side of the corridor, the atmosphere changed. The corridor was lined by a dozen doors that also had been modified—they had been fortified, with the glass pane replaced by metal bars.

Inside of these classrooms-turned-prison-cells were wolf shifters—what was left of my pack.

A YEAR BEFORE, Conri and his gang had joined forces with the Nightmist witches and invaded our pack lands.

It had been fast and hard, and we barely had time to react. Conri killed Franc, the alpha, and took over the mantle, and the alpha's son, the one wolf I thought would step up and challenge Conri for the title and save us all, had run away.

Like a coward.

And just like that, we went from a pack of about seven hundred wolves to less than fifty.

At first, Conri had them all thrown in the prison building,

beneath the town hall across the main square. They were crowded in there, without any resources.

I convinced him to have them moved. I had hoped for a house, maybe a couple of houses, but Conri had chosen the school—he had a few classrooms modified to accommodate the prisoners by taking out all the desks and materials, leaving only a few mattresses and blankets, and installing bars on the outer windows.

It was still better than the prison.

There were eight classrooms in this corridor, and about six wolves in each one of them.

Right now, they were all waiting by the bars at the doors, knowing Rue and I were coming with lunch—their only daily meal.

"It's about time," Lonan said, reaching his arm out. He was an old wolf, almost as old as Rue, but the man had hated me before, and he hated me even more now.

Rue glanced at me as I opened my mouth to tell him to shut his pipe or there was no food for him. She shook her head once and I let out a long sigh. Sometimes I wished I was heartless and willing to let them starve. If they starved for two days, they wouldn't be so mean to me.

Truth was, most weren't anymore. Not after the attack, not after I helped with their wounds, after I carried them when I didn't have any strength left, and especially not when I fought with Conri every opportunity I had to make their lives a little easier.

"Just shut up, Lonan," Roman said from the classroom across the hall.

The old man grumbled but retreated from the door.

I shot a thankful glance at Roman and he offered me a tight smile. Once upon a time, Roman had been a friend. The night of the attack, he had tried helping my mother and me, but Phell hurt him. I thought he had died, but thankfully he recovered.

Mealtime went like usual: Rue and I stopped in front of each classroom's door, we passed the paper bowls and cups to the wolves inside through the gap in the bars, then moved on to the next door.

In the beginning, the wolves tried rebelling and leaving their classrooms. They rammed against the other door, as if they could break it down. Once, they even used me as a bargain to have Conri let them go.

Nothing worked.

Conri had only made their lives worse.

Eventually, they stopped trying to break out.

They knew there was nothing we could do.

I knew that.

But deep down, I hoped that someday, somehow, I would be able to free them. To have them go back to their houses and restart life the best way they could.

That was only a dream.

I handed the plate to Jay, our healer apprentice, and he nodded at me. "Thank you, Miss Raika," he whispered. Every time I looked at him, I pitied the boy. He was probably twenty years old like me, but he looked fifteen because he was skinny and he cowered into himself all the time. But our healer died during the attack and he was all we had. Thankfully, no one had gotten seriously ill in the past year.

I smiled at him. "You don't need to call me that. Just Raika is fine."

"I know, Miss Raika." He sat down on the classroom floor and turned his attention to his food.

I shook my head and moved on.

"How's life on the top side?" Lucille asked when I stopped in front of her classroom.

I stared at her—even knowing they took showers once a week, she was still pretty. Her blond hair wasn't as brilliant and voluminous as it once was, her skin wasn't as flawless, but her hazel eyes were just as fierce.

Once upon a time, she had been a bitch who was madly in love with the alpha's son. But then he left us, she was captured, and like most of us, she lost the rest of her family ... and in the past year, she turned a little less bitchy.

"How's Minsi?" Dom asked from her side.

I frowned. Dom had been the alpha's son's best friend, and he had lost his own younger sister, so his worry about Minsi was only natural.

"She's fine," I said, my voice tight.

"Any more panic attacks? Is she still barely speaking?" He asked those things at least once a week.

And whenever he asked those questions, Tyren straightened and listened closely. He was Minsi's brother. I had tried having him moved to the house with us, but Conri wouldn't allow it.

"She—"

"Stop talking, bitch," Serge snapped from the next classroom's door. "You should be ashamed of yourself."

"Serge, stop it," Rue said. She pushed the empty cart back to the outer door. "She's the reason you get a decent meal every day."

"That's exactly my point." Serge wrapped his hands around the bars and stared at me. "Why hasn't the devil thrown you in here? Why do you live in the alpha's mansion with Minsi? Why do you have privileges no one else does?"

Good question. I didn't know it either.

"Because she's been sleeping with him," Lonan shouted from his classroom.

"She probably helped them come in," another one said and a few *yeahs* sounded from every classroom.

One year.

We had been at this for almost a year, and they still said the same nasty things. The first few times, my temper won and I yelled at them. Once, I even had a fist fight with Lucille. But she didn't believe I was involved anymore. At least, that was what she said.

Though I was able to control myself better now, their insinuations still got to me.

My fists clenched.

Rue turned to me and shook her head slowly.

I walked out of there as fast as I could. I grabbed the empty cart, pushed it down the corridors, and into the kitchen. The cart wheel caught and it turned to the side, falling to the tiled floor with a loud clank.

My shoulders sagged.

"I'm proud of your behavior," Rue said from somewhere behind me.

I faced her. "What behavior? Me sleeping with Conri?"

She glared at me. "Don't turn your anger toward me. I'm not the bad guy. No one here is." She walked past me and picked up the fallen cart. "I know you didn't choose this. I know he simply picked you from the rest, probably because you're one of the most spirited and the most beautiful of all of us, and ... I don't know. I don't know why, but I'm glad." She rested a hand on my shoulder. "If he was hurting you, then I wouldn't think so, but he's not. He grants you freedom, and you use it to take care of Minsi, of us. That's noble of you."

It didn't feel noble.

It felt like an uphill battle, one that hadn't moved an inch in the past year.

Yes, I was grateful for living in the former alpha's house instead of the school with the others. I was glad Conri had allowed me to take care of Minsi and keep her at her house.

But I didn't understand why.

He said I amused him, and that was it.

I never pressed it again, afraid that if I did, he would revoke my privileges.

"I'm sorry," I whispered.

Rue offered me a sweet smile. "What for? You haven't done anything wrong." She turned to the sink. "Now, let's clean up this mess."

Like a well-oiled machine, Rue and I fell into our routine. We washed up the pans, pots, and utensils we had used to make lunch, and we cleaned the kitchen.

When we were done, the demon in charge of Rue took her away—to another classroom outside the others. Her lonely prison.

Tomorrow, we would do all of this again.

Just like we had been doing for almost a year.

3

RAIKA

I TOSSED AND TURNED IN BED, UNABLE TO SLEEP ANYMORE, despite the early morning hour.

My guest bedroom at the alpha's mansion was better than my old home. I had a queen bed (before I had a twin one), a walk-in closet (a cheap, rickety armoire), and a bathroom (I'd shared one with my mother). I had salvaged some things from my old house—my clothes, my favorite books, a pink touch lamp my grandparents had given me when I was a child, and a portrait of my mother and me on my twelfth birthday. This was one of the few pictures we had together. She had been the quiet type, shy, a little lost inside her head, but at the same time, she had been my best friend, and I knew she had loved me.

My grandparents died years ago, but I lost my mother during the attack. Phell killed her in front of me. I had been too shocked to do anything about it at the time, but I attacked him once the massacre was over. He would have killed me if Conri hadn't stopped him.

Why had Conri singled me out? Why was I the only wolf in the pack he didn't hurt, except for the occasional slaps and insults? He didn't hurt Minsi either, but that was only because I had begged him to let me take care of her. She was having massive panic attacks locked away in the school. It took Rue and me a good three months to calm her down enough so she could go a day, then a week without a panic attack. The last one she had had been a little over two weeks ago, when I had fought with Conri in front of her. When he slapped me, she broke down.

Sometimes I worried Conri would imprison her with the others, or he would hit her. She would go down in the rabbit hole again if he did, and I wasn't sure I could bring her back this time. The girl had lost her parents in the attack. Tyren, her middle brother, was locked in the school, and her older brother, the alpha heir, had fled.

I sat up. I didn't care if it was earlier than usual. I could get a head start on my day. I had to help Rue with the pack's meal and teach Minsi. I didn't want her to miss out just because our lives had been uprooted. I wished Rue would teach her, since she was a real teacher, but Conri wouldn't allow it. I was already grateful he let her help me with the cooking; I wasn't sure I would be able to do it every day by myself.

I pulled on ripped jeans, a cropped top, and my peep-toe wedge boots. I brushed my long, wavy black hair down my back until all the knots were gone, and I applied eyeliner to enhance the blue of my eyes. I didn't care what Conri's demons and wolves thought when they saw me. I wasn't dressing for them; I was dressing for myself.

I opened the door to my bedroom and was surprised to

see no demons in the hallway. I tiptoed to Minsi's bedroom and put my ear to her door. With my faint wolf hearing, I could hear her slow, deep breathing. She was still sleeping.

But where were the demons?

Not seeing them worried me a little, but at the same I was relieved. It had been so long since I was able to walk around without being followed. The only places a demon didn't come with me were the library, my bedroom, and when I went in any bathroom.

I glanced at the other doors in the corridor. The main suite, which had belonged to the alpha and his mate—now Conri occupied it. Tyren's bedroom. And the last door in the corridor ... the alpha's heir's bedroom.

His door often called to me, but in the year I had been living here, I hadn't succumbed to that call, to my curiosity. I had never entered his bedroom. He had left us here. He had abandoned us. Left us to suffer and die. He didn't deserve my thoughts.

My longing.

A yelp reached my ears and I stilled. Hushed voices, a groan.

The demons were downstairs with Conri.

Knowing most of them were at least half-wolves, I tiptoed carefully to the stairs on the other side of the house, climbed down, and reached the kitchen. Half of the kitchen was open to the breakfast room, which had another wall open to the family room. I couldn't get farther in if I didn't want to be seen or heard.

I flattened myself to the wall closest to the opening, focusing on their words.

"... if not that, then what is your explanation?" Conri asked.

"I don't have one," Draz said. He was one of Conri's favorites but I rarely saw him around. "We've been searching for almost a year now, and we still haven't found it."

I sucked in a sharp breath.

This wasn't the first time I overheard their conversations. I had talked to Rue about it because sometimes I thought Conri had attacked our pack because he was searching for something.

"I won't admit defeat," Conri said, his voice tight. "We need to find it and soon."

"I'm doing all I can, sir. My group and I—"

"I'll assign more men to help you, but I want to see progress soon, Draz. Find a clue or a map—something!—that leads you to it." He paused. "You know what will happen if you don't."

"Yes, sir," Draz muttered.

Conri groaned. "Dismissed."

The shuffle of feet and bodies was loud and clear. I tiptoed back to the stairs and pretended I was just now coming down.

Three demons walked into the kitchen and halted when they saw me. I opened my mouth in a fake yawn and ignored them, as I usually did, while turning toward the fridge.

"Sir, Raika is awake," Phell said. My usual shadow. My mother's killer.

Damn him.

I grabbed the milk from the fridge, a mug from the cupboard, and set them down on the large marble island. And then my day was ruined when Conri entered the kitchen with one of his big smiles.

My stomach turned and my appetite disappeared.

Couldn't I at least have breakfast in peace?

"Good morning, Raika," he said, his voice upbeat. "Ready to make better choices today?"

I filled the mug with milk and put it in the microwave. "What do you want?"

"I have a surprise for you."

Oh, shit, a surprise from Conri? "I don't want anything from you."

Conri gestured to another demon to come in. The demon nodded his head, grabbed a large box from the couch, and hurried to Conri's side.

"I have an appointment tonight in New York City," Conri said. "And you're coming with me."

I stared at him, sure I hadn't heard him right.

Two feelings warred within me. I hadn't left the pack lands in so long. Most wolves left the pack lands to study and become something the pack needed, like another doctor, or a civil engineer, then they came back to live with the pack. This place was home. We were born, lived, and died here.

Before the attack, my life was far from perfect. My family had been demoted to the lowest-ranked wolves in the pack by command of the alpha many years before I was born. We had been shunned, scorned, and bullied. There were times when I wished I could leave.

But no one could without a specific order from the alpha. The previous alpha had hated my family with every inch of his soul, so I had been sure I would never leave.

Until now.

But why did Conri want me to come with him to some appointment? In New York City? That was ... so far away! Besides, I didn't want to go anywhere with him, even if that meant leaving the pack lands for a while.

I also couldn't leave Minsi behind.

"You're nuts." I gave him my back and reached for the ground coffee in the cupboard.

I never touched the knob on the cupboard's door.

Conri's hand closed around a good chunk of my long hair and pulled it down and toward him. I did my best not to yelp and let him know how much that hurt.

"I don't think you understand, little wolf. I'm not giving you an option. You *are* coming with me." He pulled my hair more, forcing me closer. I gritted my teeth and endured the pain in my scalp, in my neck for being twisted in an awkward angle, in my chest for being this close to the devil. He sniffed at me, almost touching his nose to my cheek, making my insides recoil in disgust. Conri jerked his chin toward the demon with the box. "Take that to her bedroom." He looked at me again. "That's your dress. Be ready at noon."

He let me go and I braced my hand on the island, doing my best to contain my rage. There were sharp knives in this kitchen. I could easily cut him.

Kill him.

But then I was sure his wolves would kill me, kill Minsi, and probably kill the rest of the pack.

"What about Minsi?" I asked at his retreating form.

"Rue will stay with her," was all he said before walking away.

I grabbed the mug with both hands and counted to ten ... fifteen ... thirty. I almost threw the mug at his back. It would only get me in more trouble.

Not hungry anymore, I dumped the milk in the sink and put the mug in the dishwasher. Since my morning was ruined and I wouldn't have much time to finish my chores before having to leave with the devil, I needed to start ASAP.

I went upstairs and woke up Minsi so she could have

breakfast and we could start her lessons—with demons following our every step.

4

SHANE

I buttoned up the dark green shirt and glanced at myself in the full-length mirror. I looked good as hell, but when I stared at my eyes for too long, I could see past the mask I wore all the time.

For the longest time, my pack, the Nightshade, had been allied to several other packs in the region, and also to a local witch coven—the Nightmist witches. We had always joked the similar names was a sign, that our alliance was unbreakable. But almost a year ago, after a misunderstanding, the Nightmist witches turned on us. Along with wolf-demons, they attacked us by surprise.

And killed my entire pack.

My father, my mother, my younger brother and sister. My friends.

My mate.

Sick as they were, the witches took me to their coven and left me to rot in their dungeons. In the beginning, they tortured me, but after a while, they seemed to forget I was there. For days, they would fail to feed me.

Closing my eyes, I shook my head.

No, it didn't do well to dwell in the past.

About six months ago, I had been rescued. I now lived in DuMoir Castle, where the most powerful vampire coven on this side of the globe resided. Witches were here too, all part of the Silverblood coven, because Lord Drake, the leader of the vampires, was mated to Thea, the Witch Queen of the Silverblood witches.

They had welcomed me without question, and I would always be thankful for that.

Killian and Lavinia, the vampires who had orchestrated my rescue and helped me get away from the Nightmist witches, also lived here, and they had become my good friends.

And tonight, they planned on taking me to a hidden supernatural nightclub in New York City because I needed to relax a little—according to Lavinia. I teased her, saying she hadn't been watching me. I had been flirting with many of the females in the castle, and whenever there was a party, I danced and charmed a handful of them. I was relaxed.

"That's what you want everyone to think," she said.

Well, apparently I wasn't fooling everyone as I first thought.

While at DuMoir Castle, Lord Drake had assigned me roles like anyone else who joined the coven. I often patrolled the forest behind the castle with Killian, though I always shifted in my wolf form for that.

Once or twice, Lord Drake had asked me to talk wolf shifter business with him, but I told him no. I didn't want to know anything else about wolf shifters, even if I was still one. I wanted to live here, do the job I was assigned, and forget the past.

A knock came from my chamber's door.

My lips tugged up. Chambers. Though the house where I grew up had been big, I had never lived in a castle before. I called this place my bedroom, or suite since it had an adjacent bathroom ... but here everyone said "chambers."

All right, it was cool living with these vampires and witches, but there were things that would be hard to get used to.

I opened the door and showed Killian and Lavinia my cockiest grin.

Lavinia rolled her eyes. The beautiful vampire had been a witch not even six months ago, and somehow she had retained her witchy powers after turning. A rarity, according to all.

Killian narrowed his eyes at me. "You're not flirting with my mate, are you?"

"Maybe," I teased. "Why? Are you afraid she'll leave you for me?"

Killian slapped my shoulder—harder than needed.

"Ready to go?" Lavinia asked.

Nodding, I stepped out of my chambers and closed the door behind me.

With a wicked grin of her own, Lavinia sauntered down the hallway.

"What's up with her?" I asked Killian as we followed his mate.

"It's also her first time going to a supernatural nightclub."

I frowned. "How many have you been to?"

"Quite a few, but ... not in the last twenty years. Who knows what has changed since then?"

I nodded.

Prince Killian of DuMoir Castle had been locked inside a

magical box for twenty years. He had been lost in a monster realm, where time went by a lot slower, and Lavinia had been the one to rescue him. It had practically been love at first sight—though neither of them admitted it.

We were a little over two hours north of New York City, but the trip in Killian's new Porsche Taycan had been smooth and fast—so far, I hadn't met one vampire who respected speed limits.

The club was located in Manhattan, off Broadway Avenue. A conspicuous six-floor parking garage building at street level. We parked there and then a set of secret elevators in the back of the garage took us below ground to the club's main entrance.

The elevators opened to a large room with a beige stone floor and a wooden sliding door on the other side, where three huge men stood. If I had to guess, they were either demons or some other kind of supernatural.

As we approached them, Killian flashed them a golden coin—stamped with the same W that was on the sliding door.

One of the demons took the coin and pulled the door open.

Beyond it was pure darkness. And no sound.

"Are we in the right place?" I whispered.

Killian nodded. Holding hands, Killian and Lavinia stepped into the darkness. Curious, I went in after them and stepped onto a landing. Beyond the landing, the nightclub stretched on forever. Down a set of stairs, the space opened and a huge crowd danced to music that boomed and shook the floor and walls. To the right, a long bar disappeared in the vastness of the place. To the left, round tables and stools dotted the edges of the dance floor, and beyond that, low couches lined the wall.

In the back, a set of wide stone stairs led up to balconies overlooking the dance floor. The VIP areas. I wondered how you got one of those. The most powerful of the supernatural, the privileged? All Killian had to do was use his title and he would be given the best of the VIP areas.

Killian and Lavinia led us to the left toward a familiar face at one of the round tables—Twyla. The shadow fae had spent twenty years in the monster realm and Lavinia had rescued her when we escaped the Nightmist witches. It had been a mess, but we had all made it through.

And now Twyla was here with her mate, Daleigh, Lord of the Frost Court in the fae realm. We greeted them like old friends, but Lavinia and Twyla left us to dance. Even though the guys' attention was on their mates, they made for good company—quiet, serious, not too curious. We ordered drinks and loaded french fries and made small talk.

I appreciated them inviting me, but I felt like a fifth wheel. Twyla said she had tried reaching Ariella, a fallen angel with a long history with DuMoir Castle and their friends, but couldn't. Ariella was on a mission to recover her wings from the demons who took them, and she was often unreachable because of that.

At some point, the guys went to the dance floor with their mates and I was left alone at our table. I was glad for the break. I didn't need them babysitting me all the time.

I glanced to the side, trying to guess everyone's species. Wolf shifters weren't the best at that unless we could smell them, and even then, it could be tricky. But here, with the heavy scent of alcohol, perfume, and sweat, it was impossible.

A group of girls caught my attention to my right. One of

them, a brunette, smiled at me and I couldn't help but smile back. It was automatic at this point.

The brunette batted her lashes at me, and I let my smile turn wolfish. Her friends poked her and she shook her head at them. I strained my hearing, but with the loud music and incessant chatter, I only picked up a few words.

"... go ..."

"... he's cute ..."

"... have fun ..."

After taking a long sip of her drink, the brunette rounded her table and walked toward me.

"Mind if I join you?" she asked, touching the empty stool beside the one I occupied.

I gestured to the stool. "Please do." She was prettier up close with small, hazel eyes and pink-painted lips. I leaned closer to her. "Tell me, you and your friends are vampires, right? That's the only explanation for how pretty you are." Her cheeks turned red. "Oh, I see you aren't."

She stared at me for a moment, being coy or pretending.

Just like I was.

Like I always had most of my life.

This girl was pretty and it was fun to flirt, but despite all the rumors going around DuMoir Castle, I hadn't taken any woman to my bed. Or men for that matter.

I wouldn't start now.

"Actually, we are—"

A shadow moved several feet behind the girl and something in my gut tightened. I rose from the stool to take a better look. The shadow, now with more shape, weaved between the tables and stools, walking away.

Long, wavy black hair, average height, slim but with the right amount of curves, especially under that tiny black dress.

She glanced over her shoulder, to the VIP area upstairs, and I got a side profile of her face.

Fair skin, high cheekbones, delicate nose ...

I stopped breathing.

It couldn't be. I had to be dreaming.

A pull tugged deep inside my chest. My heart hammered against my rib cage, and I almost lost my shit when she disappeared from my sight.

"Hm, what's going on?" the brunette stepped in front of me.

Shit, I had forgotten all about her.

"Excuse me," I said, but once again, she was already gone from my mind.

I glanced around, desperately trying to find her.

Because it was her. It had to be.

Even though I knew she was dead.

My mate.

5

RAIKA

I PULLED DOWN ON THE BLACK DRESS, TRYING TO COVER MORE of my thighs, but it was impossible. This thing was short and too damn tight. The worst part was that it was a great dress for a night out; I was just upset it had to be like this.

Wishing I could be anywhere but here, I grabbed a glass from the silver tray on the low table among the leather couches and turned to the metal railing. I drank a sip of the champagne and looked down at the throng of supernaturals dancing to the beat of the music.

Some were easy to identify. Fae with their pointy ears, goblins with their short height and greenish skin ... but most, it was hard to guess. I saw a happy group of young women dancing together, a couple of males in their midst, and I tried making out what they could be. Vampires? Witches? Warlocks? Wolf shifters? I didn't know.

But they all seemed happy, like they wanted to be here with their friends or mates, or whatever ... having a good time.

My situation was entirely different.

I brought my glass to my lips and paused. No, drinking wasn't a good idea. I couldn't get drunk while out with Conri. He had respected certain boundaries so far. I wanted to make sure he would continue to do so.

I dropped the glass back on the table and stole a look at him.

He promptly smiled at me, raising his glass at me.

I frowned, looking from him to the two men seated with him—I couldn't be sure, but I thought they were wolf shifters, from one of the packs around the Nightshade. I bet if Lucille was in my place, she would have known who they were, but since I had never been invited to any pack event, I didn't know anyone's faces.

Did they know what was happening to us? To my pack? Did they care? Or were they plotting with Conri to conquer more packs?

Disgust rolled in my stomach.

I let out a long breath and glanced to the dance floor again, trying to distract myself with other thoughts. Like the fact that I was in New York City! I had read about the city in books, but I never thought that one day I would be here. Honestly, though, it barely counted. Conri had chartered a private jet to fly us from Prince Albert to New York. We arrived at a small airport where a limousine waited for us. I had seen a little of the city from the windows, and I even recognized Times Square and Broadway Avenue.

I just wished there was something—

An idea struck me as fast and hard as lightning.

On the way here, Conri had mentioned that humans who knew about our world were able to enter the club, but it was rare. Which meant, all these people dancing, drinking, and laughing were supernaturals.

Someone here could help me.

But who? And why?

Why would a stranger help me?

I hated the thought of working with witches, since all of my pack's problems started with them, but who better to help me? To concoct a potion, a poison I could slip into Conri's drink, into his gang's drinks? I didn't have any money on me, but the alpha and the betas had been rich. There was money in my pack. If only I found a witch willing to make a blood pact with me. I could promise to pay her once Conri and his gang were dead.

It was risky. It was crazy. It was rushed.

But this was my only opportunity. When would Conri let me out again? In another year? No, I didn't have time to think this through and come up with a better plan.

It was now or never.

Inhaling deeply, I turned to the VIP area's exit.

Promptly, Phell and Gunner stepped in my way.

"I'm going to the restroom," I told them. I pointed to the end of the hallway that connected all the VIP booths and areas. There, right beside the stairs leading down, was the women's restroom.

Gunner went to Conri and whispered in his ear. Conri glanced at me, then nodded. He gestured to the demons, probably telling them to stay glued to my ass.

The first clue that I hadn't thought this plan through.

It didn't matter. I still had to try.

I walked out of the VIP area, my stomach tight, my heart speeding up. This was nuts, this was insane, and yet I couldn't stop myself. It felt like a shot of adrenaline in my veins.

I entered the restroom and the two demons trailing me waited outside. I went to the mirror and looked at my face.

My blue eyes gave away my anxiety, my excitement, and my fear. I schooled my expression into a scowl.

To pass the time, I reapplied the red lipstick over my lips and smoothed down my dress, checking to see if I hadn't gotten it dirty or smudged anywhere. The two occupied stalls opened, the women washed their hands and left. Then another one came in.

All right, it was time.

Slowly, I opened the door and spied out. Phell and Gunner were a handful of feet away from the door, standing like statues along the wall.

Two women more came in and I stepped back to let them pass. The first woman washed her hands. She would leave. I needed a plan.

I smiled at her. "I like your hair."

She looked at me through the mirror. "Thanks." The purple streaks shimmered and changed into red ones.

"That's amazing."

"It's my thing."

"You're a witch?" What were the odds I would find one in here? Was I that lucky?

"No, I'm a fae." She brushed her hair back and around her ears. Oh, now I saw it.

"Cool. What kind?"

"Blaze fae. My hair is actually a burnt orange, but I like playing with glamours."

"That sounds like fun."

The other two women exited the stalls and washed their hands. I opened my mouth, ready to ask them if they were witches, but that felt way too creepy. However, they saved me the trouble when one of them smiled at her reflection in the mirror, showing off her fangs.

"Are you all friends?" I asked, knowing the answer.

One of the vampires shook her head. They headed to the exit. I moved with them. The fae moved too. I kept my voice low but asked other stupid questions, making them talk to me, while we all walked out the bathroom together. I somehow was able to keep myself among the three of them, and I pretended I was fixing something on my dress's hem so I could keep my head low.

I needed three seconds.

The staircase opened at my feet and I dashed down, not even saying bye to the three females I had used to my advantage. Hopefully, the demons hadn't seen me and thought I was still in the restroom.

At the bottom of the stairs, I paused for a second and took a deep breath.

So this was what freedom smelled like?

I almost laughed since all I smelled was cheap perfume, sweat, and booze.

Despite my brief moment of respite, I knew this freedom wouldn't last long. The demons would realize I was taking too long in the restroom and they would come after me.

I didn't have much time.

I had read enough fiction books about the human world and the ones who depicted nightclubs sometimes mentioned someone in the corner or along the back walls selling drugs. I doubted it would be much different here—a witch selling potions for supernaturals who were willing to pay for a good brew or spell that enhanced their experience.

I weaved among the round tables on this side of the club, my head darting around, looking for someone who fit the bill. I got closer to the back wall where low couches were and—

Bingo.

A woman sat on one of the couches, several small vials with colorful liquid in front of her. A man seated beside her got a blue vial, paid her some handsome amount of cash, and left.

I sat in his vacated spot.

"What are you looking for, dearie?"

"Actually, I want something different," I told her, my voice trembling. By the moon, I hoped she would help. "You see, I need something stronger."

The witch smiled at me, revealing yellowed and crooked teeth. "The black vial, dearie. That's the strongest I have. But be careful. If this is your first time, it might knock you out for a couple of hours."

I shook my head. "No, I don't want a potion. I need something to knock out a half-wolf shifter, half-demon ... permanently."

Her dark eyes rounded. "You're looking in the wrong place, dearie." The amusement was gone from her voice. "I don't sell those kind of potions."

"But what if I pay and—"

"You didn't hear me, dearie. I won't sell you anything."

My stomach sank. "Then point me in the right direction. Someone who can help me."

"You don't understand, dearie. You won't find anyone here. If a witch, or anyone else, is found with that kind of potion, we'll be in violation of the club's rules and that gives the owner the right to kill us on the spot. No one is stupid enough to try."

I stared at her.

No, there had to be someone. There was always someone

doing illegal things. Which was terrible, really, but right now, I didn't care.

For the first time in almost a year, I had seen a glimmer of hope.

I wasn't ready to let go yet.

"But—"

"No buts, dearie." The witch's expression changed. She shooed me off with her wrinkly hands. "Now leave. My next client is waiting."

I wanted to argue with her, to beg her, to offer her my life in exchange for a solution, but I didn't think she would change her mind. I stood and stepped away, freeing the space for her next customer.

My breath hitched and the hope in my chest died.

No, I couldn't be done yet. I held on to the hope with both my hands and looked around. Someone else here was probably selling potions. Even if they couldn't sell the potions I needed now, maybe they had something for later. I would figure out how to get it, how to pay them for it.

I walked between the low couches along the wall and the round tables, my steps slow and unsure, searching for witches. The problem was, almost everyone in here looked devious, and I had no way of knowing who was a witch unless I asked.

I reached the end of that area and paused. To my left was the entrance. My heart squeezed. I could run. Then I could find a witch or someone to make the potion I was looking for. Or I could find someone to help me attack Conri and save the Nightshade pack. Maybe the other wolf packs in the area. There had been a handful of them before, but I hadn't heard anything about them since Conri took control.

But what about Minsi? And Rue? And the others? If I left

like this, who would make sure Conri didn't hurt Minsi, didn't kill the others?

I pressed a hand to my aching heart.

A force hit me so hard, my breath whooshed out of my chest. In one second, I was standing there, pondering about my ill future, and the next, I had my back against the wall, two hands on either side of my head, and a looming figure caging me in.

I swallowed a yelp and died on the inside, sure it was Conri. He had found me and now I would be punished for my behavior.

Then I stared at the face inches from mine.

My breath caught.

No, it couldn't be.

But it was.

I hadn't seen this face, this body, in almost a year, but there was no denying it. Dark brown hair cut short around a fierce face and sharp features. I had always thought his jaw and chin could cut stone. Smooth, olive skin, thick eyebrows and deep, chocolate-colored eyes that stared at me as if he was seeing a freaking ghost.

Shane.

The alpha's son who had fled and left his pack to die.

Minsi's older brother.

And my mate.

6

SHANE

THE MOMENT I FOUND HER STANDING BY HERSELF ALONG THE wall, watching the entrance, all thought fled from my head.

I practically rammed into her, spinning her around and pressing her back against the wall. My hands splayed on either side of her head. I caged her in, because I was sure this was an illusion and I had to get to the bottom of this before it disappeared.

Raika's light blue eyes rounded. "Shane," she whispered. My name on her lips was like a knife to the gut. By the moon, I fought my self-control, but I lost.

I embraced her so damn tight. I pressed my nose to her neck and hair, inhaling deeply. Moon above, how I had missed her warm jasmine scent.

Raika stood frozen in my arms, but then she brought her hands up and shoved hard against my chest.

I let her go, but I didn't step back. "Raika, I—"

"Stop!" Her eyes turned fierce. "I don't want to hear it. I don't even want to know what you've been doing, you coward!"

I frowned. "What?"

"Return to whatever hole you were buried in and stay there." She attempted to step away from me, but I wasn't having it. I placed my hands on either side of her again. "Let me go!"

"Never." The words were out before I made sense of them.

"What? You left us to die!"

"Left you to die? What the hell are you talking about?"

Raika scoffed and crossed her arms, pushing her breasts together and up. That tight dress, that low cleavage … I was having a hard time looking at her face.

"You know what you did."

"Apparently, no, I don't."

"Is this some kind of sick game?" Her eyes brimmed with unshed tears. "When the Nightmist witches attacked the pack with Conri and his gang, you fled. Conri killed your father and you didn't even try to win the pack back. You put your tail between your legs and ran. Like a coward."

I stared at her, sure I hadn't heard her right. "Wait. That wasn't what happened. Conri used his alpha command."

She shook her head. "That night … it's a jumble in my head. I don't remember details."

That night had been pure terror and chaos. I doubt any of us did. "Regardless, that's a lie. Who told you this?"

"Lie? Here you are, aren't you? Free, happy, dancing in a damn nightclub."

"So are you!"

"I'm not here by choice, coward. I'm here because Conri wants me here. And—"

I snarled. "Conri? You're here with Conri?" Wait … He had killed everyone from our pack and kept my mate alive? Why? Was she his woman now?

A ball of fury grew in my gut.

"Didn't you hear me?" Raika brought her arms up, and for the first time, I noticed the bracelets around her wrists. Only they weren't bracelets ... "It's not my choice. I haven't had a choice since you fled and left us behind."

Was he ... was he forcing her to be with him? I touched the thin cuffs disguised as bracelets to match her outfit, and Raika promptly lowered her arms. I knew what those were. I had worn those same cuffs for six months. I hadn't been able to turn into my wolf form with those. Even my strength, my healing, my hearing, and my sense of smell had been affected.

It wouldn't be different for her.

If Conri wanted to, he could use those to bend her will.

I clenched my teeth and breathed out slowly before I either punched the wall or went after that demon.

But something else registered in my mind.

Left us ... "Do you mean other Nightshade wolves are alive?"

"Why are you doing this? Pretending not to know anything? You think this is funny?"

"Nothing about this is funny." If only she knew how much my chest hurt right now at seeing her, at finding out she hadn't died last year. By the moon, my fingers itched to touch her again. "Raika, you have to believe me, I didn't know."

She shook her head. "You don't need to come up with excuses, Shane. You don't owe me anything. You made your choice. Your freedom, your happiness over your pack. Over your own sister and brother."

I stilled. "What did you say? My sister? My brother."

"Ah, now you care? Don't worry, I'm taking care of them."

"Minsi and Tyren are alive?"

"Oh my God, Shane, stop." She pressed two fingers to her temple. "Here's the deal: take a step back and let me go. I'll pretend I never saw you here and you can go back to being oblivious to everything. You can continue to enjoy your freedom and not care about your pack, while I go back there and try to make everyone's lives less miserable." I didn't understand. What had happened that night that our stories, our experiences, didn't line up? "Besides, you never really cared about me. No need to start now."

All right, that one was on me.

I let out a long sigh and ran a hand through my hair. Raika tried moving when my arm was gone, but I pressed my hand against the wall again, keeping her right in front of me. If it depended on me, she would never leave me again.

I wished I had had the guts to do that a year ago when the mating bond snapped. Or even before that, when my soul and my heart called for her. Deep down, I had known she was my mate since I first laid eyes on her when were kids on her first day in school. I remembered how beautiful she was, how fierce and energetic. I had been ensnared into her web long ago and she had no idea.

"That's not true," I started, ready to finally tell her everything from my perspective. "I—"

"Shit." Raika clasped my shoulders and pulled me to her. "Duck!" she yelled.

I ducked. A whoosh swiped above my head. My instincts kicked in and I whirled, my wolf fangs showing.

Three humans stood in front of me, their eyes pitch black. No, not humans. Demons. Conri's lackeys.

And they were here to take her.

Over my dead body.

The demons charged me. My claws extended, black fur

covered my skin, and I met them head-on. One demon went flying backward, slamming into a group dancing and knocking over a table and stools. The others seemed stronger. A blow struck my face from a second demon, but my claws ripped through the flesh of his bicep, almost taking off his arm. The demon recoiled, holding his cut arm.

The group who had been dancing joined the fray, diverting the demon's attention from us. I reached for Raika behind me ...

But she was gone.

My chest constricted and I scanned the area, trying to find her in the confusion. It took me five desperate seconds, but I saw her. Across the growing fight around me, being dragged by the arms by two demons. She jerked against them, but with the cuffs on, they were too strong for her.

Rage burned inside me.

I started after her.

The three demons were back, and the fight around us became bigger and wider. The music stopped, the lights came on. Security personnel ran among the guests, breaking them apart.

Shifting half of my face, I bit down on the neck of one of the demons and ripped out his throat. His body fell at my feet. The other two didn't even blink as they came at me, intent on killing me.

But they never touched me.

Killian and Lavinia were there, holding the demons back. They sank their fangs into the demons' necks, killing them instantly.

A witch threw magic bombs at the crowd, trying to disperse them. Killian and Lavinia approached me and we retreated. On the way out, we found Twyla and Daleigh.

Most supernaturals in the nightclub were leaving and the chaos was almost as bad on the outside. For a moment, the parking garage was flooded with people and cars. The supernaturals spilled onto the sidewalk and Broadway Avenue, causing humans to scream and run. Cars stopped or sped away.

I had no idea how the club owner would clean up after this mess.

But I didn't care.

Worried about just one thing, one person, I halted by the sidewalk a few feet from the confusion and searched.

My friends came to my side.

"What happened?" Killian asked. "Who were those demons?"

I shifted my face and arms back to normal. "Those were Conri's lackeys."

"Conri?" Lavinia frowned. "Who's Conri?"

"The half-demon, half-wolf who massacred my pack." Only, that wasn't entirely true, was it? Not all of my pack had been killed that night.

Minsi, Tyren, and Raika were alive.

"What?" Twyla's eyes bugged. "What were they doing here? How did they find you?"

"I don't think they were after me," I told them. I stared at my friends. They didn't know the entire story. It was too painful to tell, even to remember it. "I think they were guarding someone else."

The demons seemed protective of Raika. I tried reasoning, but all I could think was that she was at a nightclub with Conri's demons, wearing that damn sexy dress. Did she have some kind of deal with Conri?

My chest hurt. Perhaps she was his woman now.

No, it couldn't be. Could it?

"Who?" Lavinia asked.

I swallowed, still having a hard time believing it myself. "My mate."

Killian stared at me as if I had grown an extra head. "What?"

Right ... I had never told them about my mate.

To be honest, I had only told my mother about Raika.

I felt defeated. I had lost her long ago, but tonight, I had lost her again.

7

RAIKA

I didn't even see Dixon and Phell coming for me. My attention had been on Shane fighting the other three demons.

Dixon and Phell grabbed my arms and hauled me away while Shane was distracted, while the entire club was. A bigger fight erupted around Shane, and the supernaturals, some incredibly prone to violence, didn't hesitate before fighting people they didn't know just for being pushed.

I opened my mouth to call for Shane, but I shut my lips. I didn't want to say his name, not when Dixon and Phell could report back to Conri. At the stairs, I glanced back once and briefly met Shane's eyes. He was absorbed in the fight, his arms and half of his face shifted into his beautiful black wolf.

Then, I was upstairs and Conri waited for me, rage written all over his face and body. The moment the demons pushed me to his side, Conri wrapped a tight hand around my arm and pulled me with him as he guided us to a backdoor.

In no time, we were inside the rented limousine. We left

the parking lot seconds before the supernaturals spilled outside, bringing the fight to the human world.

Once more, I glanced back.

But I didn't see Shane again.

I looked up, wishing I could get a clear view of the sky, but lights and Manhattan's skyscrapers blotted out the stars.

I still couldn't believe I had found Shane. He had been right here, and he had seemed glad to see me. Or was that my imagination? The bastard. I had been so mad at him for the past year. I still was. After all, he had been at that nightclub, having a great night out, while me and his siblings and the rest of *his* pack suffered.

So selfish.

My hands shook; my heart beat fast. It would take a while for me to calm down after this encounter.

An encounter I should put out of my mind. Shane didn't deserve one ounce of my brain power. One inch of my heart.

He didn't deserve anything from me.

When we were inside the chartered flight and up in the sky, Conri got up from his seat and gestured for me to stand too. The demons scattered to the corners of the airplane, leaving the main cabin for us.

Oh, this wouldn't be pretty.

"I'm tired," I told him, closing my eyes and leaning my head back.

"I'm not asking." He unbuckled my seat belt, grabbed my arm, and hauled me to my feet. "Where did you go?"

I jerked free from his grip, but held my ground. "To the restroom."

Conri's eyes turned red and his hands shifted into his dark-gray claws. "Don't fuck with me, Raika. You evaded

Dixon and Phell, and they found you downstairs." He stopped right in front of me. "What were you trying to do?"

"Nothing," I lied. "I wanted a moment to myself without your lapdogs following me around."

Conri gritted his teeth, several of them elongated and sharp. "I know you better than that, Raika." He snapped his teeth less than an inch from my cheek. I did my best not to flinch. "Dixon and Phell said a man was talking to you. Who was he?"

I shrugged. "I don't know. He was crazy drunk and thought I was some long-lost girlfriend, poor guy."

I barely had time to brace my core as Conri's closed fist met my stomach. The air fled my lungs, the pain spread like an avalanche, and I fell to my knees.

Conri grabbed a fistful of my hair and pulled me up again. I swallowed the yelp that wanted to break free from my lips. He held me close to him, his teeth once more a hair's breadth from my face, his foul breath filling my nostrils.

"I gave you a night away, and if you behaved, I planned on taking you out more. But you were a bad girl, Raika." He punched me in the gut again, and this time, when my knees gave away, he held me up by my hair. Tears filled my eyes. "Here's your punishment: tomorrow, the entire pack doesn't eat. I want to see you explain to them why."

He dropped me and I fell to the floor.

His claws and the red of his eyes gone, Conri went to the front cabin, probably to get a drink.

And I had a minute to wallow in my pain and hurt pride.

A sob lodged in my throat and I pulled myself back to my seat, where I lay against the window, closed my eyes, and did my best not to cry.

WE ARRIVED BACK at pack lands around five in the morning. Thankfully, Conri didn't come into the house with me. He stayed out and walked away, the moon knew where. I could only hope he went to the lake on the north side of the pack lands and drowned himself.

Everything was dark and quiet as I made my way through the house, Phell following me several steps back. He stopped at the top of the stairs and let me go the rest of the way by myself. I hated the demon, now more than ever because he had dragged me back to Conri, but at least he wasn't in my face all the time.

With a sigh, I glanced at Minsi's bedroom door. I could hear her deep breathing from behind the closed door but what I really wanted was to check on her, take a peek, make sure she was all right. But since I could also hear Rue's breathing and heartbeat coming from one of the guest bedrooms, I knew she was probably fine. Rue always took good care of her.

My eyes shifted to another door.

Shane's.

Reason warred with my heart. No, I shouldn't go in his room. But I wanted to.

Since seeing him at the nightclub, my emotions were raw and I felt like my mind spun without a direction, and my heart hadn't slowed down yet, not completely.

Despite knowing better, I went to his door, opened it, and walked inside.

His scent, still heavy in here, hit me like an ocean wave— that minty and musky scent that had always called to me.

Fate could be so funny.

My family was the pack's omega, the lowest of the low. We had been ridiculed, laughed at, turned away, and more. Shane hadn't been much different.

My mother had tried sheltering me as much as she could from the pack, but once I was five, the alpha ordered me to attend school.

"Every wolf needs to learn our ways," he had said. At least, that was what my mother told me. "I won't have dumb wolves in my pack."

But I did remember my first day at school. The pack wasn't large, always averaging about five hundred wolves, so the school wasn't big either.

I walked in the school and I was bullied by my new classmates. During lunchtime, the bullies were relentless. I had been pushed into a corner, and even then, they didn't leave me alone. Some threw lettuce and pieces of fruit at me. At five years old, and having been told to endure it since I was born, I lowered my head and stayed there with tears in my eyes.

Shane, who was two grades above mine, came to my table. I had never seen him up close before, but I knew who he was.

The alpha's oldest son.

The alpha's heir.

He had been so handsome as a child, but behind that hid cruelty. He grabbed my arm, shoved my tray into my arms, and told me to go eat by myself in the classroom.

"Right, because she's too low to eat in the same room as us," someone behind him said. I didn't remember who, but those words had stuck.

Knowing I couldn't retort to the alpha's son, I walked away.

That had been the first of many nasty encounters. But each time Shane was close to me, every time he talked to me, I felt a tug inside my chest, something that lured me to him, despite his nastiness.

I hated that feeling and I did my best to ignore it.

As I grew up, I stopped being quiet when bullies harassed me. I had gotten into a lot of trouble because of it, but I wouldn't cower. I was the lowest-ranked wolf in the pack, but that didn't mean they could treat me like trash.

I was a damn wolf like the rest of them.

Years later, we found out why I had felt attracted to him the moment we met. We were mates.

And no one besides us knew.

Shaking those memories away, I flicked the switch and the lights came on. His room was as I imagined: large, with a queen bed; two nightstands; a chair and desk with a broken laptop and a few books; a dresser with picture frames; and other decorations, all in dark wood tones and dark blue accents—the bedding, the chair's cushion, the drawn curtains. Two doors to the right led to the walk-in closet and the bathroom.

His things had remained untouched.

I walked closer to the dresser and looked at the picture frames—Shane with Mace and Dom; another one of the three of them with Lucille. And one of Shane with Tyren and Minsi. He wasn't looking at the camera, but at his siblings. The love in his eyes shone through the paper.

If he had loved them so much, why did he leave them here?

Shane seemed confused about Minsi and Tyren, about me. But why?

I shut the door on my thoughts.

I wouldn't let this moment, this hiccup, derail my mind and heart. Nothing had changed. Shane was still out there, carefree and happy.

I held on to that thought and filled my heart with anger again.

Better anger than hope.

8

SHANE

I KNEW WHERE RAIKA WAS GOING, WHERE CONRI WAS TAKING her. Back to the Nightshade lands. My pack lands.

My first instinct was to follow them, challenge Conri, and take my pack back—whatever was left of it.

But that was a death trap. If I couldn't simply challenge Conri; he wouldn't follow wolf shifter rules. He would cheat, either using the help of the Nightmist witches again or his demons, and I would lose.

And this time, instead of being imprisoned by witches, I would be killed.

I couldn't help my pack if I was dead.

So I did the next best thing I could think of: I went back to DuMoir Castle, where a certain vampire lord seemed to know a lot about every supernatural in North America.

Before we left NYC, Twyla and Daleigh had asked if they could help me with anything. When I told them I was good, they portaled back to the fae realm. But on the way to the castle, Killian and Lavinia weren't buying it.

As Killian drove, he kept glancing at me in the backseat through the rearview mirror.

"So you have a mate," he said. "Why didn't you tell us about her before?"

I shrugged, my eyes fixed on the few stars in the sky not obscured by ambient light. "I thought she was dead. It didn't seem important."

Lavinia twisted in her seat, staring at me with her big hazel eyes. "You told us the Nightmist witches along with some other wolves attacked your pack. They killed everyone and took you. What changed?"

I closed my eyes and I tried to see details I had missed before.

The Nightmist witches had been our allies, but during Minsi's birthday party, when they had been invited for a magic show, a drunk wolf assaulted one of the Nightmist witches and almost raped her.

The witch killed him, his mate killed the witch, and our alliance was severed.

The witches kidnapped Minsi, but they couldn't leave the pack lands without the alpha allowing it—that was how the barrier worked. They hid in the forest and we went after them.

During the chase, I ran into Raika. She and Minsi had a special bond. They had become friends despite the age difference. Minsi had always been quiet and shy and anxiety prone, and I knew Raika was good for her. She was one of the few people who understood Minsi and cared for her.

I had been torn. I wanted her away from the mess. Safe and sound.

Before I could ask her to leave, we saw the witches, but we

hid in a rock fissure, our bodies pressed against each other, our faces only inches apart.

That was when the bond snapped.

And I kissed her.

Or tried to. Our lips had barely touched when the witches moved on and my father found us a couple of minutes later. We sprang apart before he noticed anything, and because he hated Raika, he sent her back to town, while I joined him.

I wanted to go after her, but I had to find Minsi. We could sort this mating thing later.

My father and I found Minsi, then other pack wolves joined us, and we rescued her ... and in the process, we killed a handful of witches. And they killed a bunch of wolves. The forest floor was stained deep red.

My father offered them a deal: He would open the barrier and let them go, but the decades-old alliance was over and the witches shouldn't come back. Ever.

The witches agreed and left.

A week later, before I could figure out what to do with Raika and our bond—because if my father found out she was my mate, he might kill her—the witches came back with Conri and his lackeys.

The attack happened so fast, we barely had time to react.

Conri killed my parents in front of my family and me. I went for him, but Conri used his alpha command to stop me. To stop all of us.

The fighting restarted. I was separated from my siblings and Raika, and Conri handed me on a silver platter to the witches. They dragged me away while I saw my pack being slaughtered and the town burning to a crisp.

Later, when I was in the cell, with the thin metal cuffs around my wrists, I learned Fabula had asked for Conri's help. Conri agreed to help her kill everyone as long as he could have the pack lands for himself—kill everyone, but me. The witches wanted a new toy for their torture sessions.

I always thought Conri and his demons had reigned alone inside the pack lands, and that they had wanted the place because the barrier made it the best place to hide.

Building up on my beliefs, the witches often teased me about being the only one left in my pack, as if that was amusing. Because I had seen the fire, I had seen the slaughter, I never doubted them. Though, their words made my pain raw each time.

Little did I know that not everyone from my pack had been killed and that they had become reluctant wolves in Conri's pack.

But knowing this hurt almost as much as thinking they were all dead.

"I just saw a ghost," I snapped. "Besides what I saw and the lies the witches told me, I don't know what changed."

Instead of snapping at me, Lavinia reached back and rested a hand on my knee. "Don't worry, Shane. We'll figure out what's happening and we'll help your pack."

I stared at the black sky again.

When we arrived at DuMoir Castle, I thought I would need to wake up Lord Drake. Though this was a vampire coven, they had changed their times and routines to daytime, to match the witches who lived in the castle. Now, the vampires slept through the night.

But Drake wasn't asleep. After one of the guards told me he was awake, I barged in Lord Drake's office, with Killian and Lavinia hot on my heels.

Drake was seated behind his large desk, a glass full of red liquid in his hand, reading a thick stack of papers.

"Shouldn't you be sleeping?" Killian asked.

Drake raised his eyes green to us. "I couldn't sleep." He patted the stack of papers. "Too many reports to read." He shifted his gaze to me and frowned. "Shane. What happened?"

"What do you know about the Nightshade?"

Drake leaned back on his chair. "Your pack?" Of course he knew. I nodded. "I've tried telling you several times in the past six months, but you made it clear you didn't want anything to do with wolf shifters and werewolves business anymore."

"Just tell me," I said, my voice tight.

"All I know is that the half-wolf, half-demon who attacked your pack, and killed them all, is still there."

"Conri."

Drake nodded. "He has a large following, several supernaturals like him, and lone wolves and demons who he's collected over the years. The deal he made with the Nightmist witches was that once they killed everyone, he would stay and take over what the pack lands."

"Why? Why did he want my pack lands?"

"I don't know," Drake said.

"I want to take my pack back," I said.

Drake's brows curled. "You want to take back your pack lands? I understand your feelings, but you'll be a lonely alpha and—"

"I ran into someone from my pack," I told him.

"His mate," Killian added.

Drake's eyes rounded. "Your pack is alive?"

"At least a few of them are," I told him. For a moment there, I thought Drake had known about this but hadn't told me. But I could see now, he was as surprised as I was.

"I ... I didn't know. I'm sorry, Shane. From the report I got after following the witches and trying to assess Conri and his demons from outside the barrier, I thought your pack was all gone."

"It's the barrier," Killian said. "It nearly impossible to know what's happening in there."

True.

But now I knew my pack was still in there. I couldn't just sit here and do nothing.

For an entire year, I had believed what I had seen when being dragged away from the pack lands: the screams, the blood, the fire. I had seen so many bodies on the ground, I had believed they had all perished like that.

But I should have known better.

For the last six months, I had told myself it wasn't worth it to go back there just to see it all destroyed. That first sight had broken me. I had barely recovered. A fresh one would break me again, and I didn't think I could recover from that.

So I stayed away. I stayed with the vampires, living a half-life.

How foolish of me.

"I want my pack back," I repeated.

Drake nodded. "I understand, but with the barrier, we can't just launch an attack on them. It'll be a massacre."

I knew that. "We need another plan."

"Agreed," Drake said. "Let's gather more intel. I'll send some vampires to scout the area. The other packs are eager to talk with us, so we'll meet with them as well. They are worried about Conri's power."

I closed my hands into fists as the rage and the wolf rose inside me. It would be so easy to let it out. But that wouldn't solve anything. I reined my temper in as best as I could.

I remembered when Lavinia had been taken by warlocks not long ago. Killian was going crazy inside the walls, but there wasn't so much he could do, that any of us could. This was the same situation. I couldn't barge into the pack lands alone—that would be suicide—and the barrier prevented a head-on attack.

We needed a real plan, and we needed time to pull it off.

Time. I reminded myself that Raika and the others had been there for over a year, and they had survived. They could survive a few more days.

I had to believe that.

"All right," I said through gritted teeth.

"I'll let you know as soon as we have something," Drake said. I nodded, muttered my thanks, and marched away from him. "Shane."

I halted and looked over my shoulder.

"If I had known, I would have told you sooner."

"I know." I stepped out of his office. Once I was in the hallway, Killian and Lavinia caught up with me.

"Hey, are you okay?" Lavinia asked, resting her hand on my arm. "Do you want to talk about it?"

"There's nothing to talk about." I shook my head. "This was ... a crazy night. I'm tired. I don't think I can sleep, but I think I really should lie down and rest."

Killian narrowed his eyes at me. "If you need anything, let us know."

"Sure," I said.

This time, when I walked away, they didn't follow me.

Once I reached my bedroom, I packed my bags.

I was leaving this damn castle and taking matters into my own hands.

9

SHANE

DuMoir Castle had plenty of ownerless vehicles—cars, SUVs, trucks that could be used by anyone at any time. I picked a nice black Maserati. As I drove to the airport, I tried not thinking about it all, otherwise I'd lose my temper.

I still couldn't believe I hadn't questioned what I had seen. That I had allowed those damn witches to trick me. They had lied to me and I had believed it like a fool. Confirming my entire pack had been killed and the entire town had been burned was another way for them to torture me.

If only I had known earlier ...

I wanted to be mad at Lord Drake for not knowing about this, but the truth was, it was my fault. The ache of the loss and the months of torture had left me feeling hollow, broken in a way that was difficult to piece back together. But I had found a big piece last night—the spark that would fuse the pieces and make them whole, make me whole.

I couldn't change the past, but I could change the future.

Before I left, I helped myself to some potions. I grabbed a new one Lavinia had learned from her friend, Evelyn.

Lavinia and Killian would kill me when they realized I was gone, but after the battle with the warlocks and the Dark Devils' coven six months ago, they deserved a break from the fighting. This was on me. Drake said he would send vampires there to assess the situation, but I wanted to see it my own eyes.

Besides, they wouldn't be able to cross the barrier.

I hoped I still could.

I arrived at the airport, left the car there so someone from DuMoir Castle could pick it up later, and took a late flight to the Saskatoon International Airport, the largest airport near the pack lands. I rented an off-road Jeep and drove it north until I saw the first inn by the road.

I didn't want to sleep, but I had to force myself to rest. I hadn't slept in almost forty hours. If I continued like this, I would collapse before I even reached my destination.

I had underestimated how tired I was—I passed out as soon as I lay in the bed, and woke up hours later, right before the sun was up. I took a shower, changed, grabbed something to eat from the inn's breakfast room, and jumped on the road again.

The sun rose, shining down on this beautiful land. Being May, it wasn't as cold as it could be, and the green grass and flowers of spring extended for miles, alongside snow-topped mountains, and crystalline lakes.

My tension only increased the closer I drove to the pack lands.

It was past noon when I was five miles from the barrier. I drove the Jeep off the road and parked it between a pair of thick evergreens. If Conri's lackeys patrolled this far out, then there was a chance the Jeep would be seen, but I hoped that Conri wasn't that smart.

I took off my clothes, rolled my pants, and tied it to my ankle, then shifted into my black wolf. I ran toward the barrier.

A normal person or supernatural wouldn't be able to tell where the barrier was, or even notice where the landscape changed. At some point, the roads ended and the green landscape seemed to engulf the earth. Rocks jutted out from the ground here and there, small streams appeared, and the trees thinned.

A seamless path big enough for a large SUV appeared between the trees.

The barrier.

After listening for other wolves or demons—there was no one here—I ran toward it. I braced myself, expecting the barrier to stop me.

I passed through it.

My wolf lips tugged up in a triumphant grin, but I wiped that away from my face. There was no time to celebrate. This was just the first step.

In wolf form, I made my way toward the town.

Twice, I heard Conri's demons nearby, but I evaded them. Hopefully, they didn't notice me, and if they did, they thought it was some of the wildlife in the forest.

I couldn't pretend this place wasn't special. The Nightshade lands were a paradise. The flowers always bloomed, the water was always fresh, the grass was always soft, and it was always a nice warm temperature.

I paused at an outcropping of rocks overlooking the town. Half of it looked like a sack of charcoal had spilled on the ground, and the other half looked like a ghost town. I focused on the intact structures. The houses, the buildings, the roads, the flowerbeds lining the streets, everything abandoned and not cared for.

A pang cut through my chest.

Once more I felt guilty for not knowing, for not helping sooner.

I shook my head and moved toward the main square, hiding behind buildings and narrow driveways between houses. I stopped at a picket fence that had a good view of the main square.

Empty, abandoned. I could see demons in front of the school, and when I focused, I could hear voices coming from inside—my pack, or what was left of it. I glanced around, but saw and heard nothing else.

Curious, I weaved deeper into town, to the other side, where a lonely road took me to my old house.

More demons patrolled the house's lot from the outside. I went around the lot, until I was back in the forest and hid among the trees. Here, I had a good view of the large glass window that made up most of living and dining room's walls. And behind those, I had a partial view of the breakfast room and the kitchen.

My stomach twisted in knots when I saw Conri seated in my father's favorite chair in front of the fireplace.

Conri, the demon who killed my father, my mother, who took my pack ... the urge to rip his throat open was so damn strong. But a handful of demons lined the walls, plus the ones outside. I wasn't sure I could take them all by myself.

I forced myself to stay put.

So far, I had seen two dozen demons around town, patrolling the forest, and in the house. But I bet there were more. Conri and two dozen demons couldn't maintain this kind of control over my pack, could they? Well, I didn't know how many wolves were still alive, and they all probably had the magical cuffs, just like Raika. They couldn't fight or shift with those.

As if I had conjured her with my thoughts, Raika walked into the kitchen. By the moon, I had forgotten about her style and how good she looked—a black mini skirt, boots that came up to her knees, and a tight tank top. She looked delicious, and I wondered if the demons noticed ... if Conri did. Of course they did.

The question was, had they respected her?

Raika turned to someone behind her. She put her arm over someone's shoulder and turned to the fridge.

My heart stopped.

Minsi.

Holy shit, my little sister had grown in this past year. She was slightly taller, going to Raika's shoulders now, and her brown hair was longer and wilder. But even from here, I could see she had retreated into herself. Her shoulders sank in and she barely lifted her head.

Two demons stood in the back of the kitchen, as if they were Raika's and Minsi's shadows. Did they follow the girls everywhere?

Raika let go of Minsi and grabbed a few things from the fridge—sliced bread, cheese, lettuce. Minsi picked up the mustard and mayo ... they were making a sandwich.

But where was Tyren? Didn't Raika say he was alive too? Wasn't he in the house with them?

I swallowed a snarl when Conri stood from the chair and went to the kitchen. He stopped so, so close to them. My insides hardened and I had to dig my claws into the ground to stop myself from protecting them.

Conri said something and pointed at Minsi. My sister recoiled, her hands shaking, and she dropped the mustard. It fell on the floor and exploded, sending mustard down the island's side and to Conri's pants and shoes.

Instantly, he advanced on Minsi, his hand turned into a claw in a second.

I took a step forward …

Raika put herself in front of Minsi and pushed Conri away. She yelled at him. He yelled back. I couldn't make out the words from here, but I could hear the anger and frustration in them.

Raika didn't back off. She held her ground.

And Conri slapped her.

Fury bubbled in my gut and I took two steps forward.

One of the demons patrolling the backyard turned in my direction. I plastered myself to the bushes again and held my breath.

Damn it.

Everything in me screamed to kill the bastard for yelling at the girls, for intimidating Minsi, for hitting Raika. He was as good as dead. I would kill him, but I needed more time.

Conri yelled at them and marched away from the kitchen.

If he was interested in Raika, then he was doing a poor job of caring for her. The bastard would lose his hand for slapping her.

Conri barked something to his demons and most of them followed him—the other two stayed back with Raika and Minsi—as he exited the house and took the front path to the main road.

Meanwhile, Minsi stared at the mess and shook like bamboo on the wind, and Raika let out a breath and centered herself. I could see it took everything in her to turn and show a reassuring smile to my sister. She wrapped her hands around Minsi's shoulders and helped her sit at the breakfast table. She sat beside Minsi and talked to her, her face close to Minsi's, her hand on Minsi's arm.

When Minsi seemed calmer, Raika pushed a book toward Minsi. The biggest bookworm, Minsi delved into the book and disappeared into a fantasy world. And Raika stood, took another deep breath, cleaned up the mess, and made them some sandwiches, all the while with a brave face.

My heart warmed. My mate was taking care of my sister. Raika had protected Minsi against a demon-wolf, and it wasn't the first time. She seemed so damn strong, and that was so damn hot.

But I could see it was exhausting to her. I wanted to lend her my strength. Together, we would take Conri down and free everyone. Things would never be the same again, but we could make them better.

Back at the club, I entertained the crazy idea that Raika was into Conri. That she had become his woman. After all, why else would she be out at a nightclub with him? The idea wasn't gone yet, but now I wasn't so sure.

Right after sunset, Raika took Minsi to the basement—to the game room. It was a huge room spanning the entire house's first floor with a giant flat screen, leather recliner couches, video games, a pool table, a foosball table, a pinball machine, and some other arcade games. It was one of my favorite places in the entire pack lands, and Tyren agreed with me. Because Minsi wasn't into games, we ended up building a bookshelf in a corner for her so she could have her own library at the house, and she could spend more time in the same room as us, even if we didn't interact a lot.

I bet that was where they were headed now.

As I expected, the demons followed them downstairs.

That meant the first and second floor of the house were empty. The timing was good, and when the patrols turned away from the backyard for a minute, I raced toward the house.

I shifted on the porch, but didn't bother putting on my pants. I drank one of the potions I had stolen from DuMoir Castle—one to mask scents—then I slid the glass door open, snuck in, and headed upstairs, careful with my steps so the demons and the girls couldn't hear me walking above their heads.

I climbed the stairs that led from the mudroom to the end of the hallway upstairs. I paused in front of Tyren's bedroom door. It was closed, but I couldn't hear anything coming from the inside. I opened the door and spied in—the place was dark and smelled stuffy as if it hadn't been open in a while. Where the hell was he?

I followed Raika's jasmine scent and entered my bedroom. It was exactly the same as I remembered, but now I could smell Raika's faint scent in here. Which meant she wasn't sleeping here, but she had been in here recently.

I didn't have time to think about that now ... I went back to the corridor and found her scent was stronger in front of the only guest bedroom on this floor—the others were on the third floor. I opened the door and her scent wafted over me like a drug. Damn, she smelled good. I knew it was because she was my mate. She probably didn't smell this good to other wolves, but still, I could drown in her scent and die happy.

The room looked the same, except for a few additions—a

new portrait of Raika and her mother, a stack of romance books, a glass of water, and some other little things.

My mother had always kept the guest bedrooms stocked and ready, so I knew where to find what I wanted—I opened the nightstand drawer and picked up the notebook and pen in there.

I scribbled a note and shoved it under her pillow.

Then, I ran out of the house and into the forest.

Now, I waited.

10

RAIKA

I stayed with Minsi in her bedroom until she fell asleep. Seeing her in her bed, her breathing steady, her face finally so peaceful, brought a sense of peace to me.

It was the only moment I relaxed.

But it was brief.

I walked out of her bedroom and saw Dixon and Phell at the end of the corridor—it worked to shatter the illusion and throw me back into this infernal reality.

Raging on the inside, I walked into my bedroom and closed the door. Without turning on the lights, I sat on my bed and took a long breath. It came out in little sobs, but I swallowed the tears that wanted to come out.

I wouldn't cry. I was stronger than this. I had endured this situation for a year. I had kept Minsi and the others safe for just as long. I wouldn't break down now.

I wouldn't break down. Ever.

Because Minsi and Rue and Tyren and all of the others depended on me.

I took a quick shower to wash away any memories of this

damned day and put on my pajamas—shorts and a tank top. Tired but restless, I lay on my bed and tucked my hands underneath my pillow.

I touched a piece of paper. Sitting up, I pulled the paper from under my pillow. I turned on the lamp on the night-stand and stared at it.

Meet me where we found out about us.

I reread the damn note at least ten times.

Shane was here? He had been inside my bedroom? How?

I shot from bed and glanced out the window, into the forest behind the house. From here, I couldn't see anything, but it was dark out and a handful of demons patrolled the outside at all times. If Shane was out there, he wouldn't be close to the house.

I turned to my closet and paused.

What the hell was I doing? Shane had abandoned us, and now he was here? The will to leave him hanging warred with the will to run to him and find out what he wanted.

The latter won.

I put on black shorts, a cropped black top, and black boots—wedge ones, since it would be easier to walk in the forest with those. I picked up my leather jacket, tied my hair into a ponytail, and stopped again.

From the top of my nightstand, I picked up my long metal nails. My mother had given them to me many years ago when the bullies started turning physical. She said she didn't care if we ended up in trouble later, I wasn't supposed to let anyone hit me.

Thankfully, after I scratched Lucille's arm with the metal nails once, the bullies stopped trying to hit me. They pushed me here and there, but their bullying turned psychological.

Still, I carried those nails everywhere. Especially after

Conri had taken over and brought me to live here. I wasn't sure what he wanted from me, but I thought he wanted to have his way with me, to force me to sleep with him. If he did, I would either kill him, or kill myself.

Thankfully, besides the few scratches I had given Conri, I never had to use the nails against him or any of the demons. I pocketed the metal nails.

Then I paused again.

How the hell would I get out of this house?

As silently as I could, I opened my bedroom's door and spied out. Dixon and Phell were near the stairs, their backs to me. I couldn't go out that way, but there was another place. Grateful demons didn't have the same hearing wolves did, I tiptoed to Shane's bedroom. I opened the door, slipped in, and closed the door. I went to the glass door and slid it open enough so I could sneak onto the balcony, then closed it again. I crouched down and stayed low behind the wooden rail, watching the patrols.

When the two walking around the estate disappeared in opposite corners, I didn't think. I scaled the railing, swung my legs around, and lowered myself, holding on by my arms. When I was as low as I could go, I jumped down softly. This would have been easier if I could shift, but right now I was glad that we had lots of physical education and basic fighting and survival skill classes in school; otherwise, I wouldn't be strong enough to do this.

I ran into the forest and disappeared behind the trees.

Knowing Conri had patrols in the forest, I stopped and listened. The crickets and a gentle breeze rustled the leaves. I trudged to the southeast edge of the forest, where a rock formation jutted from the ground. The witches had hidden here with Minsi when they kidnapped her. However, on the other side of the rock formation, there was a fissure and that was where Shane and I had hidden.

And where the mating bond had snapped.

I slowed even more at the fissure's entrance.

"Shane?" I asked, my voice low.

Wearing only dark jeans, Shane walked out from the fissure.

I took a step back and swallowed hard.

Dear moon ... I was mad at him. I hated him with all my heart. But right now, all I could think was how hot he looked. His dark brown hair framed his sharp, almost cruel face, his dark eyes boring holes into mine, his expression dangerous. The moon peeked from between the trees, like a spotlight shining down on his wide shoulders, strong arms, chiseled chest, and washboard stomach. He even had that damn V that disappeared in the low hanging jeans, along with a faint patch of dark hair below his navel.

I took another step back for good measure and placed my hand inside my pockets. "What are you doing here?"

He matched my step, coming closer. "Raika ..."

I slipped the metal nails in place and brought them out, my hands like claws. "Stay where you are."

Shane frowned. "What are you doing?"

"Is this some kind of trap? Are you working with Conri?"

"What?" He raised his hands in peace. "What the hell are you talking about?"

"I don't know, you answer me. You left us to rot, to die, for an entire year, and now you suddenly appear right when Conri takes me out. It's like he found you and is now rubbing my nose in your freedom."

Shane's jaw popped as he gritted his teeth. By the moon, I

had forgotten he did that when he was mad, but was holding it in ... and it was sexy as hell.

In a flash, Shane rushed to me. He knocked the nails from my fingers. I tried punching him, but he pushed me back and twirled us around, until my back was against the rock formation.

"I'm not working with Conri," he snarled, his face so close to mine. "I want the demon dead." He tilted his head to the side. "But ... I confess, I thought you were his woman."

I almost choked. "W-what?"

"You were all dressed up and at a nightclub with him. When you first told me you were there with him, I thought he had killed everyone and kept you for himself. And you had let it happen."

I pushed him hard on the chest. "Are you insane? I would rather die than let him touch me."

Shane moved half a foot back but kept too close for comfort. "Then why were you there with him? Why are you at the house while the others are at the school?"

I crossed my arms. "It's none of your business."

His gaze flashed to my chest before settling on my face again. Men.

"Raika, I'm trying to talk to you, damn it." Shane ran a hand through his hair, his arm tensed, his muscles strained. "I saw when he hit you earlier this evening. Are you okay?"

My eyes widened and I pressed a hand to my cheek. It didn't hurt anymore, but ... "You saw? How?"

"I was at the forest's edge. It was so damn hard to stand back ..." He shook his head. "Thank you. For protecting Minsi."

"I didn't do it for you." He knew Minsi was my friend long

before this mess started. I had always cared for her and always would.

"I know," he muttered. "What happened to her? She seemed even quieter than before."

I didn't answer right away. I didn't think he deserved an answer, but this was his sister. "After being kidnapped, having her parents killed in front of her, and having her brother abandon her, Minsi started having panic attacks. It was bad and it freaked out everyone."

"Holy shit." He clenched his fists. "And what about Tyren? I didn't see him at the house."

"He's at the school with the others," I told him. "Because he wasn't as bad as Minsi, Conri wouldn't let me take him too."

"What do you mean, not as bad as Minsi? How bad is he?"

"He's fifteen, Shane. He's a teenager and living in a cell with four or five other wolves. And he also suffered and saw everything Minsi did. He's closed off but in a teenage-rebellious way."

"Damn it. I have to help them," he said, his voice low.

"Shane, I'm helping them as best as I can."

"I know, I know, but ... Raika, I think there's a big misunderstanding about what happened the night our pack was attacked. You seem to think I abandoned you—"

"Then how do you explain what happened?" I asked, my voice bitter. I hated him, even when my core, my soul, my heart yearned for him. I shook my head, reminding myself that was the bond. Not me. Not my real feelings.

He leaned into me again. I fought not to glue myself against the rocks behind my back. "I was spelled and taken by those damn witches. I saw the town burning as they dragged me away. Later, they confirmed my fears, saying Conri and his demons had killed all of you and burned the town to the ground. There were no survivors." I stared at him, stunned. He went on. "The witches kept me in their dungeon where they tortured me, and—" He pressed his lips shut. He walked into a patch of moonlight coming from a gap in the trees. He opened his arms wide and I gasped. He still had the tribal tattoo that snaked across his side and up his chest, but more than that, now he had dozens of small scars across his torso, around his shoulders.

My fingers itched to reach up and touch them. "Dear moon," I whispered.

He lowered his arms and stood right in front of me again. "Six months ago, I was rescued from the witches, and I didn't come directly here because I thought there was nothing left … that there was no one left. If I had known, I would have come back right away."

I stared at him, into his dark eyes. I wanted to hate him. I wanted to call him on his lie, but deep down, I knew he was telling the truth. "That sounds horrible."

"It was, but you know what was worse?" His hand moved toward me, but he lowered it. "Do you have any idea what it felt like to see you again? To find out you're alive?"

All right, now he was pushing it. "Why are you doing this? Don't pretend you care."

He flinched as if I had slapped him. "I care—"

"No, you don't." If he cared, he wouldn't have pushed me away the moment the bond snapped. When his father found us a few minutes after, instead of telling his father about it and standing by me, he told me to run back home and hide. He had been ashamed to be mated to the lowest-ranked wolf in the pack. And that rejection, that knowledge, hurt almost as much as the rest. Pride welled in my chest and my temper rose. "You don't care about me; you don't care about your pack. You might care for Minsi and Tyren, but that doesn't seem to be enough, does it?"

"What the hell are you talking about?"

I lifted my chin. He had rejected me. Now it was my turn to reject him. "We don't need your help, Shane." I wanted to make him suffer like he had done to me. "Go back to where you came from and stay away from us."

I pushed him back with all the strength I had. I crouched down to pick up my discarded metal nails, and fighting against the constant pull of the bond, I ran.

RAIKA

I BARELY SLEPT THAT NIGHT. HOW COULD I, KNOWING THAT Shane had been in my room, that he was outside in the forest on pack lands?

Early in the morning, I got up, got dressed, and started breakfast. Today was a special day and I wanted to make a special breakfast for Minsi. With Phell always watching me, I baked a lot of cinnamon apple muffins and made hot chocolate for two. I placed one of the muffins on a white plate and topped it with sweet frosting and a pink candle. With the plate and lighter in my hand, I went to Minsi's bedroom.

I thought I would have to wake her up, but when I pushed her door open and stepped in, I found her seated on her bed, hugging her pillow, her eyes red.

I put the plate and lighter on the side table and sat beside her. "Oh, Min." I pulled her to me. "Why are you crying, sweetheart?"

She didn't say anything. I didn't think she would, but I knew why she was crying. It was her eleventh birthday and the one year anniversary of when everything changed.

I smoothed my hand down Minsi's back. "You're fine now. No one can hurt you anymore. I won't let them."

A sudden need to tell her about her brother hit me, but what good would that do? Minsi was already suffering. If I told her that her disgraced brother was back and taunting me —and that I had told him to leave—it would only make her suffering worse.

Holding Minsi now, I wondered if I had been too harsh on Shane. If I shouldn't have told him to leave.

No, I wasn't harsh. I had given it to him the same way he had given it to me. Hard, cold, and true.

We didn't need his help. I would find a way out of this, even if it killed me.

"How about this: Let's go downstairs and eat your breakfast. I made something special for you." I pointed toward the cupcake on her nightstand. "And then we can spend the rest of the day at the library ... and no studying. We'll just read and talk about books." I still had to cook and feed the pack, especially because yesterday I hadn't and they probably wanted to kill me, but that should be quick. "Would you like that?"

Minsi turned her face to me, her eyes shining with tears. "Yes," she whispered.

My heart squeezed. That had been her first word in days, maybe even weeks.

I kissed the top of her head and helped her up. "Let's go."

<hr>

THANKFULLY, the rest of the day went a little smoother. Minsi put on a pink skirt and white shirt I had found in her closet, and she allowed me to make her hair into a braid-tiara, with the rest loose down her back. She looked pretty, and after that good cry and hug, she seemed a little lighter.

She ate two muffins for breakfast, and we took the rest with us to the library—I would take some of them to the school. We settled on the rug and pillows in the middle of the library, and true to my word, we ditched the schoolwork and read fiction books. Minsi was reading a middle-grade series about dragon riders, and I started a new contemporary romance—I so needed a dose of non-supernatural in my life.

But after the first four chapters, I put the book down. It was great, but the romance was making me itchy because my love life was a mess.

I glanced at the bookshelves around us, my thoughts returning to Shane. I couldn't stop thinking about him as much as I wanted to.

Sometimes, I thought we had been wrong that night at the fissure. Whatever we felt wasn't the mating bond. It was just some kind of lust induced by having his naked body pressed against mine, the tight space, his scent clouding my judgment. It had to be.

I sighed. It was the mating bond, though. I knew that because of the way I felt whenever I was around him, how there was an invisible line pulling me to him, how I couldn't not want him, even though I should hate him.

Why did fate have to be so cruel? Why did I have to be mated to him? Why couldn't I have been mated to another low-ranked wolf? Someone who hadn't been mean to me my whole life. Like Roman? Or maybe no mate at all! That would have worked too.

I left when it was time to meet Rue in the school's kitchen. I took the muffins with me, one for each, and a handful more for whoever wanted seconds. Lonan kept saying I made the muffins to shut them up so they wouldn't be mad at me anymore for making them miss one day of food. But Tyren, Lucille, Dom, and some others remembered that it was Minsi's birthday ... and the one year anniversary of when this mess started. In a couple of days, it would be the one year anniversary of the attack that killed most of the pack and turned the rest of us into prisoners.

I didn't argue with Lonan, or the other wolves who decided to agree with him. They could think whatever they wanted because I knew the truth. Without me, Conri would have left them to die.

After cleaning up the kitchen, I went back to the library and spent the rest of the afternoon with Minsi. This time, I grabbed a crime book ... I needed some justice in my life.

Here and there, I made a comment about a book or a movie—old ones, since we hadn't seen any new movies in a year now. Ever since taking over, Conri controlled the TV remote at the house, and he destroyed most of our devices—phones, tablets, laptops. We had no way of communicating with or knowing what was happening in the outside world.

Minsi barely talked. She said another two or three words, and that was it.

Before the sun set, we made our way back to the house—with Dixon and Phell at our backs. As we entered the house, I looked at the forest behind it ... was Shane still there? Watching over us? Over his sister?

It didn't matter.

We walked into the house and halted in the foyer.

Conri, dressed up in a fine suit, waited for us at the family room. "There you are! Happy birthday, little Minsi!" He smiled at her, and she hid behind my back.

"What are you doing?" I asked.

"Well, it's a special day, so I thought we could have dinner together."

"No, thank you. We would prefer having dinner by ourselves."

He walked toward me and it was an effort to stay rooted in my place. "I don't think you understand, little wolf. I'm not asking. I'm ordering you two to sit down at the dining table and have dinner with me."

I opened my mouth to retort, to tell him to go to hell, but I had done that so many times, and what did I get from that? A slap, a punch, a punishment. Defying him only made everything worse.

I held Minsi's arm. "It's okay, Min. Just sit by my side and I'll keep you safe, okay?"

She shook her head.

Damn it. Gently, I slid my hand into hers and pulled her to the dining room with me. Conri trailed behind us, a handful of demons following him.

We never used the formal dining room, and from the little Minsi told me, her family had only used it for special occasions. The room was separated from the family room by a rectangular archway and two steps down. The long, brown table stretched out in the middle of the space with eight high-back chairs with beige leather around it. The chandelier was a rectangular piece of old metal with fake candles. But the most impressive part of the room was the large floor-to-ceiling windows—even bigger than the one in the family room. It opened up to the porch, and overlooked the stone fireplace and bench outside. And beyond it, the forest.

If this house wasn't so depressing, it would have been amazing.

Conri took the head of the table and gestured for Minsi and me to take the seats to his left and right. "Please, sit."

I helped Minsi to the seat beside me, away from Conri. "We can stay, but she'll sit here." My voice was firm. I knew I was walking a thin line here.

Conri's nostrils flared, but he didn't say anything.

I sat down in my seat and did my best to shield Minsi from Conri's view.

Demons came in and brought our food—rare steak with undercooked potatoes. Conri devoured it, and I picked at the potatoes, but didn't touch the steak. I could eat a rabbit or squirrel when in wolf form, but steak like this? No, thank you.

Minsi didn't touch her plate.

And Conri noticed. "Why, birthday girl, aren't you hungry?"

Minsi looked down at her hands and didn't answer.

"She's not hu—"

"I asked her," he snapped, glaring at me. "Not you." He stared at Minsi again. "Answer when I'm talking to you, little girl."

Minsi recoiled.

"Conri, she—"

The devil slapped the table, rattling the plates and glasses. "Shut up!"

Beside me, Minsi whimpered. She shook from head to toe and was about to break down into a panic attack.

Conri stood and so did I. "I won't shut up." I faced him head-on. If he threatened her, he would have to go through me. "You know she's not well. She's having a panic attack and you're making it worse!"

He raised his hand to slap me. I braced myself, even

closed my eyes, but the slap never came. I spied under my lashes and Conri lowered his hand.

"Just get out of here," he snarled.

As quickly as I could, I scooped a sobbing Minsi in my arms and raced upstairs with her. This time, I took her to my bedroom and laid her on my bed. With the side lamp on and without changing my clothes, I scooted in with her and held her tight.

"Let's play," I whispered to her. "Tell me five things you can see, four things you can touch, three things you can hear ..."

Minsi didn't really say anything out loud, but I knew she was following my directions, finding the things, and making note of them in her head. Slowly, her shaking lessened and her sobs stopped.

"Just sleep." I smoothed my hand down her back. "Don't worry about anything. You'll stay in my bedroom with me the rest of the night. I'll take care of you."

Minsi snuggled her head into my shoulder and slept.

I STARED AT THE CEILING. Minsi had been asleep for three hours, maybe a little more. My arm under her head was numb, but I was so afraid of moving and waking her up. At some point, I had reached my nightstand, turned off the lamp, and tried to sleep, but I couldn't.

I couldn't do many things.

Like save Minsi, save the pack.

Not by myself.

I had been trying to come up with a plan for a year now, and what had I accomplished so far? A big, fat nothing.

I needed help. We all did. And even if it killed me, someone could help.

Slowly, I rolled Minsi to her side so I could pull my arm from under her. I had promised I would take care of her the rest of the night, and I felt bad because I was about to leave her alone, but I knew she was safe in here. The demons would only come in if there was another attack or if the house was on fire.

I made sure Minsi was comfortable, then I followed the same footsteps as the previous night and exited the house through Shane's bedroom and over the balcony.

I raced to the rock formation and the fissure as fast and silently as I could.

I slowed down when I saw the fissure illuminated by the moonlight streaming through the trees' crowns.

"Shane?" I called him, my voice low.

He wasn't here.

I called again, searching in the fissure, around the rocks, and in the cave.

There was no one here.

Shane had left.

Again.

A pain cut fast and deep through my heart. He had left me behind, and this time I had only myself to blame.

12

SHANE

WHEN RAIKA RAN FROM ME IN THE FOREST, I HAD BEEN SO stunned by her action, it took me a few seconds to react, and then it was too late. I tried going after her, but by the time I was close enough to call her, I had seen one of the patrols in the forest, and I hid.

Raika had slipped through my fingers.

Conri had told her and the others that I had left them. That I had been so afraid of confronting him that I had tucked my tail between my legs and fled.

By the moon, and they believed it? Didn't Raika know me better?

Truth was, she didn't. I might have paid attention to her for most of my life, mostly when she wasn't aware of it, but she had never paid attention to me. And if she had, what she would have seen? A cocky alpha heir with a golden spoon in his mouth.

Because that was what I let everyone see, what I let them believe.

Because that was what my father expected from me.

My father, Franc, had been a difficult man. He had been raised to be a firm and fair alpha, but he had become so much more. He had been respected by our people ... and feared.

Wolf shifters usually had red-hot tempers, but my father had won the prize for it. He yelled at others and made them feel inferior and inadequate.

He'd been the opposite of his mate, Petra, my dear mother, who had been sweetness incarnate. I had heard before that opposites attracted, and it couldn't be truer. Where he was a violent storm, she was the calm after.

She often said my father wasn't a bad man. He was too passionate about his beliefs, and when people crossed him, he had no patience for it. And he had raised me to be the same. When I was little and showed more of my mother's side, he punished me. He didn't beat me because my mother wouldn't allow it, but it came close.

Once, he locked me in my room and left me alone and without food or water for an entire day. My mother cried and begged to him to take the punishment back.

Another time, he broke my favorite toy right in front of me.

Then, he once threatened to punish Tyren and Minsi instead ...

So I learned. If I wanted him to leave me alone, to leave my siblings alone, I had to be like him.

At least on the outside.

My mother hated to see me changing like that, even if she knew it was a facade, and she often said that it was temporary. One day, I would be alpha and I could be whoever and however I wanted. I just had to endure until then.

Even if he was a bastard most of the time, I hadn't wished for my father to die. I didn't want to become alpha so young.

But even that was taken from me when the Nightmist witches kidnapped me.

Because if it had depended on me, I would have fought Conri. I would have challenged him. I would have killed him and taken care of my pack.

That was the past. I couldn't change that.

But I was going to change the future.

I went back to the Jeep hidden outside the barrier, put my clothes on, and drove to the nearest wolf pack to the south.

Because I had been raised to be alpha, I had had other classes the rest of the kids in school didn't, like politics and wolf affairs. I knew that our pack was the only one this far north in Canada, but there were five wolf packs directly south from us, and none of them had the same magical lands that we did.

I arrived at the first pack, Boldridge, and was told to turn around. The alpha wouldn't even see me. The second and the third packs, Wildtail and Warhide, let me in and talk to their alphas, but apparently they were at war with each other again. I had heard a powerful vampire coven had to step in to stop the war— Lord Drake and his vampires from DuMoir Castle. And if this war between the packs continued, Drake would bring his vampires to deal with it.

I had been told, when I was living in DuMoir Castle, that the previous lord and the coven's founder had helped many supernaturals in the United States, Canada, and Mexico, and ever since, any trouble that arose and disturbed the human world or spilled into another supernatural group, he and his vampires intervened. To maintain the peace.

It sounded noble but also entitled. Who had put the vampires in charge?

But I digressed. During my time with DuMoir Castle, they had been nothing short of honorable, helpful, and friendly.

I drove to the fourth pack, my hopes already waning. This one, Ironfang, had always been a little reclusive. They lived on a mountain and most of their houses were inside the mountain, in a series of mazes and tunnels that formed a huge underground town.

Delco, the alpha, met me in one of the short buildings at the base of the mountain, in a room that served as an office.

"Shane, alpha heir of the Nightshade pack," Delco said. He gestured to the chair across from the wide table in the center of the room. He wasn't alone in the room. His mate sat beside him, and his beta stood to the left. "Or is it? Last I heard, you had fled after the devil claimed your pack."

I frowned. "That wasn't what happened."

He leaned over the table and steepled his fingers. "Then what happened?"

Without going into much detail, I told them about the witches and I begrudgingly admitted I had no idea my pack was still alive.

"But now I know that's not the case," I said.

"No, it's not." Delco exhaled. "Things have been complicated around here. Warhide and Wildtail are at war again, Boldridge prefers to live as if the rest of the world doesn't exist, and then there's the Nightshade. The devil actually contacted me last week. He wanted to meet and talk alliances. I told him to go fuck himself, but from I heard, he met with Whitecrest."

"Conri's forming alliances? That sounds improbable."

"I think so, that was why I refused, but if he allies with another one of the packs, we might be in trouble."

"We need to get rid of Conri before he turns us all against each other," I said. "I want to challenge him, but I don't think he'll stick to wolf rules. I need help."

Delco narrowed his eyes. "You're an alpha without a pack, boy."

I gritted my teeth. I wasn't a boy, but I knew he had called me that to aggravate me. "Help me and I'll have my pack back."

Delco glanced at his beta. Something passed between them, a comment I couldn't hear, information they both knew and didn't want to share.

"All right," Delco said. I sat straighter. I had come here to beg, but deep down, I thought all the packs would turn me away. "Conri is becoming a nuisance, and it would be best if he was gone. But I won't help you out of the goodness of my heart." The alpha laughed and even his mate smiled. "I'll do this for you on two conditions. One, you present me a plan, a real plan, to take down the devil and his demons. And two, you'll owe me a favor."

Shit. I had considered that but was hoping the packs wanted to see Conri gone. I didn't have many choices here, did I?

I extended my hand across the table. "Deal."

With a sly grin, the alpha shook my hand.

And I knew I was about to save my pack to doom it again.

13

RAIKA

AGAIN, I DIDN'T SLEEP WELL. MINSI HAD SPREAD OUT IN MY bed, leaving me a tiny corner, but mostly it was because of my stupidity. I had sent Shane away and then gone after him. What did I expect to find? That he would have waited for me to change my mind? He wasn't a puppy.

After three half-slept nights, I felt like a freaking zombie, but I groaned and pushed through. Minsi, however, asked to stay in bed and I allowed her. It wasn't as if school was the most important thing now, was it? I insisted she studied so she would have something to do, something to focus on other than our brutal reality.

Quietly, I took a shower, got dressed, and went downstairs for breakfast. I did take something for Minsi to eat once she felt hungry, because I knew she wouldn't leave my bedroom today. And if she did, it would be to go to her own room. She wouldn't wander the house with Dixon following her around.

Since Minsi stayed at the house, I didn't need to go to the library with her for her lessons, so I headed straight to the school and arrived a couple of hours before Rue was allowed out of her classroom. By myself, I got a head start on lunch. Rue had done so much for me in the past few days, she deserved a break, even if a small one. Looking back, I didn't know how I had convinced Conri to let Rue help me, but I was glad I did. I wouldn't be able to handle all of this on my own.

As I washed the vegetables, my mind wandered.

What now? What were we supposed to do now? What was I supposed to do? Just go on teaching the little I knew about English, math, and history to Minsi, reading books, and cooking lunch every day? Until when? Until I grew old? Until Conri decided we were a nuisance and killed us all? I didn't understand the devil. Not that I wanted to, but ... why keep us here like this?

By the time Rue joined me, I had fresh bread baked, and a chicken and rice bake in the oven along with some roasted vegetables.

"What am I supposed to do?" she asked, looking around.

I shrugged. "Keep me company?"

But there was plenty to do. Rue and I got the paper plates and plastic utensils, and when the food was ready, we served a hearty portion to each plate. We piled those onto the cart, grabbed apple juice from the fridge, poured them into paper cups, and then took the cart to the classroom cells.

As usual, the people in there were eager for the food and most of them didn't even seem grateful for it. It was like it was my duty to come cook for them, to serve them, since I was the pack's omega. They had no idea I had to fight to be allowed to serve them real food instead of being treated to scraps like dogs.

Lonan was in a foul mood today. While he ate, he kept mumbling about Conri and me, and insinuating we were planning something together. Serge indulged him, adding fuel to the flames. I ignored them.

Tyren took his plate from Rue, not me. My chest constricted upon looking at him. He was fifteen now, a smaller, shorter version of Shane. If allowed to have a normal life, I bet he would turn out to be as tall and strong as his older brother.

I knew his anger wasn't only toward me. Shane had been his hero, or so I heard, and like me, Tyren believed Shane had left of his own accord. That he had chosen to leave us behind.

At the same time, I wanted to tell him what I had found out, even if I was having trouble believing it myself. I knew I shouldn't. Shane was gone again. Telling Tyren the truth would only make the wound fresher.

At the last cell, I served Lucille, Dom, and their other three older cellmates. Lucille leaned against the door and watched me from across the bars. "What's with that pout? I haven't seen you like that since I used to bother you."

I frowned at her. "Bother me? You bullied me, just like everyone else."

She flinched. "That's the past." She had never apologized for what she had done, for all the hurtful things she had said, and I knew she never would. There was too much pride in her personality. I was relieved she hadn't joined Lonan and Serge in harassing me even now. "Something happened?"

I stared at her and a sudden urge to tell her everything hit me hard. I had never had a friend other than my mother, Minsi, and Rue, but my mother had been my mother. Minsi was too young, and Rue had been more of a mentor and protector. I hadn't really talked to any of them.

But, like with Tyren, telling her everything now would

only bring more misery to all of them. No, I could live with this misery on my own.

"Everything is the same," I said. As normal as it could be when you lived in the conditions we did.

"How's Minsi?" Dom asked.

"Conri was a jerk to her last night. She had another panic attack."

Dom cursed under his breath.

Lucille shook her head. "He really is the devil."

"I'm glad I learned how to deal with it and help her out. She slept in my bed, though she asked to stay in today."

"Poor girl." Dom dropped his plate and punched the wall beside the door.

I took a glance at the other doors around us. "She isn't the only child here having to grow up like that." Though she seemed to be the most affected by the night of the attacks. After all, everything had started during her birthday, and she had been kidnapped by the witches.

Knowing all these kids were growing up in cages broke my heart.

I caught Tyren spying me through the bars in his cell door, probably trying to hear about Minsi. When my eyes met his, he ducked behind the wall and disappeared.

"Time to go," Phell said from the outer door. It was rare for him to speak up, but when I took too long to serve the prisoners, he always complained. Conri had probably told the demons Rue and I weren't allowed to talk to them for long.

Moon forbid that we should concoct a plan to escape!

If there was any way, I would have found out already.

"Go before you're punished," Lucille said. My eyes met

hers, and for some reason, I felt like she knew more than I let on. That I didn't hide it all as well as I thought I did.

I nodded and walked out the outer door, to the other side of the hallway. Rue was already at the kitchen, washing the pots and pans in the sink. In silence, I joined her.

After a few minutes, she asked, "How have you been?"

I paused what I was doing and looked at her. Those warm eyes set on mine, and I felt like hiding. Did she also see more than I wanted her to? Did everyone see it all?

Shit.

"I would say I'm doing okay, but that would be a lie," I confessed. "But none of us have been doing okay, have we?"

She nodded. "True. But you have been tenser than usual these past two or three days."

Since I had seen Shane alive and well at the nightclub. "I think it's just the attack's anniversary coming up," I said, which wasn't a lie. In a couple of days, it would be a full year since that fateful night.

"I know. I've been thinking a lot about that too."

"Conri wants to have a celebration."

The pan she had been washing fell from her hands and clanked around the sink. "What? Why?"

"Who am I to understand what goes on his mind?"

"He can't possibly think this sounds like a good idea?"

"He's insane—"

"Watch it," Berth said, his voice firm.

Rue and I exchanged a glance but became quiet. Last thing we needed was these demons going back to Conri and telling him we had been talking about him behind his back.

After Rue and I were done in the kitchen, Berth took her back to her classroom, and I left the school. I wanted to go home and check on Minsi, but decided to make a quick stop at the library first. I could get a couple of books and take them for her. That might brighten her up a little.

To be honest, walking in the library, knowing I was truly alone in there, also brightened me up a little. I didn't flip the switches but went around the windows and drew the heavy curtains aside. Under the curtain, the tall, narrow windows still had the blinds half turned, letting some sunlight in, but not directly over the books. I closed my eyes, stood in the light from one of the windows, and inhaled deeply, taking the lovely scent of books into my lungs.

Then, I smelled something else.

Eyes wide, I turned around.

Shane leaned against a bookshelf several feet back, away from the windows.

My mouth fell open ... for two reasons. One, he was once more wearing only dark jeans and nothing else, not even shoes, and his ripped arms were crossed over his bare puffed chest. Damn, he was so beautiful standing in the middle of so many books, with his chiseled torso all apparent, his perfect face set in a scowl. It was freaking sexy.

And oh so frustrating.

Reason number two ... "What are you doing here? How did you get in here?"

He jerked his head back and disappeared behind the shelf.

I followed him to the middle of the library, where we couldn't see any of the windows. He walked around the large rug on the floor. "I tried just dodging the demons, but that proved too hard. So I drank an invisibility potion."

I halted across from the rug and stared at him. "What?"

"It's something a friend of mine learned how to make."

"A friend ... you mean a witch?"

"Yeah, well, she's still technically a witch, but now she's also a vampire."

I shook my head. Dear moon, what was going on? So while we were all in here suffering, Shane was out there making friends with a witch who could make invisibility potions?

Jealousy whipped through me—it was the damn bond. Not my real feelings. "You left again." I had almost said *you left me again.* That wouldn't have been pretty.

"You told me to go."

"I was mad at you!" I almost yelled but lowered my voice. I didn't need Phell to barge in here and find Shane. "I am mad at you."

"All right, time to air everything out. Why are you mad at me?"

"Because ..." I pressed my lips in a tight line. Damn it. "Because you left us a year ago, because you left me two nights ago."

"I didn't leave of my own will in either of those instances. The first one, I was spelled and taken by force. The second one ..." He stepped onto the rug, erasing two of the several steps between us. "You're the one who ran from me. I tried going after you, but there were too many demons around the house."

"I went back there the following night," I confessed, my voice low.

He shook his head once. "I'm sorry I wasn't there, but I spent the next day and night going from pack to pack in the region, trying to make alliances."

My chest expanded. "Alliances?"

"Raika." Shane took two more steps toward me. I held my breath. "Hear me out. I've never wanted to leave you or the others behind. If I had known you were still here, I would have fought harder. I would have come for you the second I escaped the witches."

I frowned. "You didn't fight them?"

"I believed my pack had been killed, my home destroyed. I had nowhere to go, no one to go back to. I was alone and wished the witches would kill me instead."

I sucked in a sharp breath. That must had been horrible. My heart hurt for him. "I'm sorry."

"Not more than I am." Another two steps. There were only three or four feet between us now. His unwavering eyes held mine. "I'm here now. I'm sorry I wasn't here last night. I was busy trying to find help. I won't go anywhere until I free you, Minsi, Tyren, and everyone else."

A lump rose in my throat and I fought against tears. This was too much. "I must be dreaming."

Shane erased the distance between us. He stood in my personal space and looked down at me. "Why? Talk to me."

I glanced up at him. "This feels like a dream, you suddenly showing up and saving the day. Don't get me wrong, I want to believe it, to hold on to it with both my hands, but ... after the year I've had, I'm not willing to give hope an inch of room."

Shane nodded. Slowly, he reached for me and took my hand in his.

I let him, savoring the feel of his big hand swallowing mine, of his warm skin on mine. But then I pulled my hand free, taking a step back.

His brows curled down. "We should talk about us. About the mating bond."

I shook my head. "No, we shouldn't. There's nothing to talk about."

"Raika, you know how this works."

"Yes, I do," I snapped.

During our last year of school, we learned about mates in health class. The mating bond was normal between wolves, but at least a quarter of them never found true mates. But when the mating bond snapped, it meant the two wolves belonged together. They were two pieces of one soul, one heart. The attraction was instant and strong and almost impossible to resist. In fact, resisting was unheard of since all wolves were more than happy to find their mates and spend the rest of their lives with them.

All wolves, but Shane.

He had rejected me when it snapped.

Despite the intense attraction I felt toward him, I wouldn't give in. If he'd had a choice in this, I knew he wouldn't have chosen me. I wouldn't force him to be with me. Besides, he had always been a jerk to me, to everyone in the pack. I didn't want him as a mate either.

I took another step back. "It'll be hard to resist it, but don't worry. We can do it."

"What?"

"Enough about mating bonds," I said before I broke down in front of him. "You said you came back to help and that you went out to find help. So, how did that go?"

Shane tilted his head, his eyes narrowed. He stared at me for a while, and I felt like squirming. Thankfully, he spoke before I snapped at him again. "In the last six months, I've made some friends and I know they will come when I send word. And yesterday, I talked to Delco and he said he'll help. I need to tell him when, and he'll send wolves to us."

That was the alpha of the Ironfang pack. "So when do we attack?"

"That's the problem I'm encountering. I can cross the barrier, probably because this is still my pack, but I'm not the alpha. I can't order the barrier to let the others pass. We can't attack with our army outside the pack lands."

Damn, I hadn't thought about that. "There has to be a way around that. You were the alpha heir. Didn't your father explain to you how the barrier works?"

He nodded. "My father said that once I was alpha, the barrier would do exactly what I wanted, no effort on my part. All I had to do was think about it and it would happen."

Just like magic. In school, we had also learned about the barrier—it had been created hundreds of years ago, by the first alpha and a coven of witches. The witches owed him a gift, so they created this paradise and put a magical barrier around it, and only the alpha had control over it.

However, that control was supposed to be a secret.

"So ... if you kill Conri, you become the alpha and can get the barrier down."

"True, but if I kill Conri, his demons will attack. I can't fight them all, and protect everyone by myself. By the time my friends and our allies are here, we'll all be dead."

"Damn it."

Shane nodded. "We need to come up with another plan."

I frowned, remembering something. "Speaking of plan, I think Conri has one too."

"What do you mean?"

"A couple of days ago, I heard him questioning some of his demons, asking if they have found it yet. I have no idea what *it* is, but that wasn't the first time I heard them talking about it. It seems Conri is searching for something in the pack lands." Shane's jaw popped and his eyes darkened. "Do you know anything about this?"

"I'm not sure," he said, his voice low.

"If I could find out about it. Maybe I can eavesdrop on him again, or maybe I can change tactics. Instead of always pushing him away and yelling at him, I should pretend to turn to his side and—"

"No." Shane loomed over me again, his nostrils flared and his eyes lethal. "Do not get close to him."

I crossed my arms. "Is that a future-alpha order?"

"Raika, I'm serious." He wrapped a hand around my lower arm and held tight. "We know what he's capable of. Look at everyone he killed in our pack. If you pretend to be on his side and he finds out, he'll kill you."

And then he would kill Minsi and probably Rue too. Damn, Shane was right.

"Promise me you won't do anything stupid." He tugged at my arm. "Promise me."

The desperation in his gaze hit me hard, but I forced myself to remember he was probably as affected by the bond as I was. He didn't want it, but he couldn't control the pull toward me. Besides, I was the one taking care of his sister right now. He wouldn't want anything happening to me until she was safe.

"I promise," I whispered.

He stared into my eyes and held my arm for longer than necessary, the air tense between us.

After several minutes, he dropped my arm.

I cleared my throat. "I ... I should probably go. Minsi has been alone in the house for hours now."

"Right."

"So ... what now?"

"I'll come up with a plan and we'll put an end to this. I

don't know how long it'll take, but you have my word, it'll be soon."

His word. Did it mean something?

Not long ago, Shane had been a cocky, conceited boy who thought the world belonged to him. The man standing before me ... he wasn't the same as that boy.

I hugged myself. "What will you do? Will you leave again? I mean, until you have a plan?"

"I can't stay inside the pack lands the entire time, not if I don't want to be found out."

"I understand." I did, but that didn't stop the sudden disappointment from filling my chest.

"But I'm not leaving, not in the same way." He fixed those eyes on mine again and my breath caught. "I promise you, I'll fix this. You can count on me."

14

SHANE

Raika left first. I watched from the window as a demon followed her from a distance, and they made their way back to my house. I waited a little longer, until the demons in front of the school struck up a conversation, their attention not at a hundred percent. I took my pants off, rolled them up and tied them to my ankle, drank the invisibility potion, stashed the empty vial in my rolled pants, and felt as the potion took effect.

When I was invisible, I opened the door, stepped out, closed it behind me before anyone saw the library's front door mysteriously open, shifted, and ran out of there.

It was hard to leave Raika behind, but I had to do it. Until I had a semblance of an army with me, I had to leave her, my siblings, and the others behind.

Again.

The way she looked at me before exiting the library, it was like she was afraid I was toying with her, giving her hope just to snatch it away.

As if that was the last time she would see me.

That fucking killed me.

I ran like the wind. The invisibility potion wore off after I crossed out of the pack lands, and I continued running along the trees flanking the road.

I could have brought the Jeep, but I needed the exercise to burn off this pent-up energy and frustration. I ran twenty miles to the nearest town and shifted back when I was in front of the inn where I had rented a room under an alias. Though Conri wasn't expecting me, I couldn't risk it.

I put on my pants at the edge of the parking lot, and then walked, barefoot, to my room. Thankfully, this place was deserted and no guests or workers saw me as I went up the exterior stairs and opened my door with the keys I had fished from my pocket.

In the dingy inn room, I threw myself on the bed and stared at the dirty ceiling.

A plan. I needed a damn plan.

If I called DuMoir Castle, I knew Killian and Lavinia would come, and Drake would certainly send a handful of his best vampires, if not more. If I asked, maybe even Twyla and Daleigh would come. Add those to the wolves Delco said he would lend me ... then I would have enough to fight Conri and his demons.

But what was an army without a plan?

Until I found a way of breaking the barrier, there would be no fight, no army, no justice.

I grabbed my phone from the nightstand and checked the messages and missed calls. Since I left DuMoir Castle, Killian and Lavinia had been calling nonstop, texting me and threatening to kill me if I didn't answer.

So far, I had no energy to talk to them.

But this time I sent them both a text.

I'm fine. I might need your help, though. I'll let you know.

Tired, I put the phone down and dragged my feet to the bathroom, where I took a long, hot shower. I put on another pair of jeans, a shirt, and was about to shove my shoes on my feet, when I heard shuffling outside my bedroom's door.

I stilled and focused on my hearing.

Soft footsteps approached my room. I walked to the door, shifted my right arm, and opened the door, ready to rip someone's throat.

A figure zoomed two feet back and away from my claw.

With an arm in front of Lavinia's body, Killian frowned at my claw. "Now you're attacking your friends?"

"Shit." I shifted my arm back to normal and stared at the two of them. "What the hell are you two doing here?"

"When your friend learns his mate and his pack are still alive and he leaves without a word, you go after him," Lavinia said. "You make sure he doesn't get himself killed, and then you help him."

A corner of my lips tugged up. "Come in."

I stepped back and let the two of them inside my room. On instinct, I glanced out into the open corridor and the almost empty parking lot before locking the door again.

I crossed my arms and turned to them. "How did you find me?"

"First, you could thank me." Lavinia raised the small brown bag she had in her hands. "There isn't a decent place to eat around here, so I brought you something."

The scent of beef tacos hit my nose right away and stomach growled in response. Yeah, I was hungry.

I grabbed the brown bag from her and sat on the edge of the queen bed. "Thanks."

Killian leaned against the dresser, while Lavinia sat in the rickety chair in front of the desk. They watched me as I opened the brown bag and consumed the tacos. I hadn't had a real meal since arriving here, so this was like a piece of heaven.

"Lord Drake knew exactly where your pack is located," Killian said, answering my previous question. "When we got here, all we had to do was track you."

"Also, there weren't many inns or other places to stay in the area," Lavinia added. She frowned. "So, why the hell did you leave without telling us? You could have at least asked to take my potions instead of stealing them."

I swallowed a big chunk of taco. There was a light teasing tone to Lavinia's voice, but I knew she was serious and also a little disappointed in me.

"You could have waited until our vampires arrived to assess the situation and reported back," Killian said. "Or you could have at least invited us to come with you."

I put the rest of my taco aside. "This is my pack." I was supposed to be the damn alpha. "I needed to do this on my own."

Killian glared at me. "Bullshit. You know that isn't how our friendship works. You were there for me when I needed you, and I thought you knew that goes both ways. Besides, you're a member of DuMoir Castle now. You don't need to do anything alone."

I stood, suddenly not hungry anymore. "I know, but ... believe me, I needed to do this first assessment by myself."

I had let everyone in my pack down; they believed I had abandoned them. Coming here by myself and seeing them with my own eyes ... it was the punishment I needed to get my ass in gear. I knew seeing how things were would rock me hard and I didn't want anyone witnessing that. Now that most of my frustration was past, there was only rage. Now, I didn't mind if others saw me.

"I was going to call you soon, because you're right. I need help. I can't save my pack by myself."

"Well, Lord Drake didn't send the other vampires because we were coming," Killian said. "We'll be surveying the area with you."

"I've already done that," I told them.

The gleam in Lavinia's eyes turned sympathetic. "Tell us what you've found."

I sat down and told them everything I knew.

After the witches took me, Conri had stayed with his demons. They cuffed and imprisoned the surviving wolves, including Raika, Tyren, and Minsi. But for some reason, Conri took a liking to Raika and brought her to my house so she could live with him. I assured them Conri hadn't forced himself on her—unless Raika had lied about that. I also told them how Raika was taking care of everyone, especially my sister.

My heart filled with pride for my mate. Our pack had been so terrible to her, always treating her like trash, with the exception of handful of people—Rue, my mother, who had told me why Raika's family had been demoted, and my sister.

If my father hadn't been watching every one of my moves, I would have been another one. But I couldn't risk being kind to her when everyone else was watching, and then having my father retaliate against her and her family.

So, I pretended I didn't care.

Focusing back on the now, I told Killian and Lavinia about the other packs and how I had gone to several of them yesterday, trying to get help. Only one offered help if I repaid the favor later.

"That doesn't sound good," Lavinia said. "What if he asks you to bow out so he can be the alpha of your pack?"

I shook my head. "One problem at a time. Right now, I need all the help I can get."

Killian approached me and placed a hand on my shoulder. "We're here for you."

"Thanks." I sighed. "There's more." Next, I told them what Raika had told me. That she had heard Conri and his demons talking about finding something in the pack lands, but she had no idea what it was.

Lavinia bit the inside of her cheek. "What could it be?"

"I know what it is," I confessed. Both of them stared at me, expectant. "Long ago, the first alpha of my pack was friends with a witch coven—"

"Don't tell me it was the Nightmist witches," Lavinia mumbled angrily.

"To be honest, I don't know which coven it was, though I know it wasn't the Nightmist witches," I told them. "That alliance came much later. Anyway, the witches wanted to gift something to the alpha. They enchanted the pack lands so it would always be spring there. No cold, no winter, no super-hot summer. Flowers always in bloom, earth always rich so it would be easy to plant anything and have it grow, abundant water in the lakes and rivers, always fresh and clean. They made a hidden paradise with a magical barrier around it so only pack members could come and go—if their alpha allowed it. However, the magic required to keep this paradise going didn't come from a one-spell-and-done kind of thing. The witches hid powerful crystals in the pack lands, and these crystals keep the magic going."

Killian's brows knotted. "So, you think Conri is searching for the crystals?"

I nodded. When Raika had told me, I almost told her I knew what Conri was after, but then I stopped myself. She had already done so much for the pack, risked so much. If I told her, I knew she wouldn't sit back and do nothing. She would do something reckless, like try to find the damn crystals by herself, before Conri could. And if she got caught ... I didn't know how Conri would react to that.

"What I don't understand is how he knew about them or why he wants the crystals," I said. "No one else in my pack knows about them. This knowledge is passed on from alpha to alpha. Sometimes the alpha tells their mate if they believe their lives are at risk, so the mate can tell the heir about it."

"Your father told you," Lavinia stated.

I nodded again. "My father told me my grandfather died young. While on his deathbed, he barely had time to tell my father everything he needed to know to run the pack. My father said he wanted to prepare me better, so when I turned eighteen, he told me several things about the pack." Looking back, I could see how my father had been firm to the point of being mean. He had been a jerk, and in many instances, a bully. But then there were other moments, when he shared his knowledge with me, when he played with Tyren and Minsi, when he seemed to care. And he had always been caring and kind to my mother. The man had had a heart, but his temper spoke a lot louder.

"So you can get the crystals before he does," Killian observed.

I shook my head. "My father told me about the crystals, but he didn't show me where they were hidden. He planned on doing that later."

"Shit," Killian muttered.

"Then we need to go in there and search for them," Lavinia said.

"It isn't that simple," I said. "The alpha commands the barrier. If Conri doesn't allow you to enter, you can't cross it."

"But you were in there," Killian mused.

"Yes, and I think it's because Conri didn't revoke my access once he became alpha. Before, I had free rein. My father stopped others from leaving—" Like Raika and her family. "—but I could come and go whenever I wanted. When Conri took over, he forbade the survivors who were there with him to leave, but he didn't do anything about the ones who were killed or taken by the witches."

"Makes sense," Lavinia said. "However, this is a magical barrier made by witches." She gestured to herself. "Powerful witch here."

"Slash vampire," Killian whispered, knowing all of us would hear it.

She shot him a fake glare. "I might not be able to undo the barrier or find a way around it, but I could at least assess it. Sometimes, the magic tells a lot. If I can feel it, maybe I'll know how to break it."

"That's a good idea," Killian said. "I bet that if we ask Thea, Almae, and Keeran to come, the four of you could easily break the barrier." The three witches and the warlock had done something similar in the past. It might work.

"That's worth a try," I agreed.

"But ..." Lavinia pressed her lips tight. "Hm, the full moon is coming in a few days. Whatever we're doing, we need to do it fast."

She didn't need to remind me of that. "I know. But right now, I'm exhausted." All that running back and forth from the pack lands was getting to me. "And it's damn late."

"Of course." Lavinia stood from the chair and reached for Killian's hand. "We'll get a room for us and we'll go to the barrier tomorrow."

I nodded. They headed for the door.

"Killian, Lavinia," I said. Hand on the knob, they stopped and turned to look at me. "Thank you for coming, for wanting to help."

"We are friends," Killian said.

"We're family," Lavinia added. "If you let us, we'll always help."

They left and I sank into bed again. But this time when I stared at the dirty ceiling, a little hope snaked shyly around my heart.

Tomorrow, the three of us would inspect the barrier.

I didn't have a plan yet, but I had a starting point, and that was way better than nothing.

15

RAIKA

I FOUND MYSELF STARING OUT THE WINDOWS, OR SEARCHING the corners of each house and building to and from the school, to get a glimpse of Shane as he watched over us.

Over me.

It was silly. I knew he couldn't watch us all day, but it made me feel better.

We had to hang on a little more. Shane would find a way for us to get out of here.

Just a little longer.

After I helped Rue with the pack's lunch, I went back to the library, where I had left Minsi and her studies. I half expected to walk in and find Shane seated at the table beside her, helping her with homework. However, Shane wouldn't show himself to her yet. It was risky.

Everything was risky.

I hadn't found Shane in the library with Minsi, but he had been in here earlier. When I sat down beside Minsi to check her progress with today's geography lesson, she showed me a piece of paper.

"What is this?" I asked, taking the piece of paper from her.

She shrugged. "It was here when I arrived."

I stared at her. She had spoken six words in one sentence. I hadn't heard this much at once in a long time. I wanted to hug her, to congratulate her, but I was afraid that if I did, she would recoil inside her shell. So, I just smiled at her and took a good look at the paper.

It was a ripped piece of yellow paper. A Post-It. Frowning, I walked to the front of the library, where the check-in counter was. I moved around it and found a stack of yellow Post-Its from the desk behind the counter. Another piece of a ripped Post-It was tucked halfway inside a drawer under the desk. I opened the drawer. Office supplies filled the drawer— staples, paper clips, glue sticks, scissors, etc. What the hell? Confused, I rummaged through the supplies, moving them around.

A yellow Post-It peeked from underneath, and this one wasn't ripped.

Meet me at our place. Use the potion.

I stared at the note, my mouth hanging open. Shane wanted me to meet him now? In the middle of the afternoon? And he had left me a potion? I rummaging through the drawer until I found a small vial with an amber liquid tucked in the back.

I picked up the vial, and for a moment, I was frozen in place.

Holy shit, I was doing this, wasn't I?

I ripped the note in a dozen pieces and threw it in the trash, under several other piece of paper that had probably been there for well over a year. With shaking hands, I put the vial in my shorts' pocket and went back to Minsi. As if nothing had happened, I looked over her lesson then assigned her another chapter and a long list of questions. That should keep her busy for another hour or so. Enough time for me to talk to Shane. I hoped.

"I'll be right back, okay?" I told her.

She nodded but frowned at me when I headed to the back door. I placed my finger over my lips; she wouldn't tell anyone.

I walked into the backroom, which served as storage, and stopped at the back door. Before Conri, I had worked in the library and I had spent most of my time in this backroom, organizing books and doing paperwork. The library's director hadn't been a big fan of having the omega as an employee, but besides all the horrible things the alpha did and let others do to us, he was adamant my mother and I should have jobs.

"Everyone has to do their part," he had said. "Even the worms have a role in the food chain."

The director didn't have a choice in hiring me, but she kept me in the backroom as much as she could.

I fished the vial from my pocket, wondering what the potion did. Did I trust Shane enough to just drink a potion he gave me? Didn't I hate the guy?

I did, I hated him, but I knew he wouldn't do anything that would harm Minsi or Tyren. I tipped my chin, drinking the potion. My throat burned with its sour taste, but it was gone fast.

At first, nothing happened. Then, a few seconds later, I felt a tingling spread. I glanced down and gasped. I was invisible!

I edged open the back door and spied out. No demons in sight. Still, I was as silent as I could when I exited the library, closed the door, and walked down the street, heading toward the forest. Twice, I stopped dead in my tracks when demons on patrol emerged from between houses. They walked past me as if I didn't exist.

Adrenaline shot through my veins, and once I was at the forest's edge, I ran toward the rock formation. My muscles screamed at me, and my wolf stirred in my chest, but as much as I wanted, I couldn't shift, not with these damn shackles. I enjoyed the wind in my face, my long hair whipping behind my back. I had to slow down once, when a patrol's movements reached my ears, but I felt pretty wild knowing that even if I ran right under his nose and he heard me, he couldn't see me.

I slowed down again when the rock formation came into view. Feeling a little naughty, I rounded the rock with slow, sure steps, watching from a distance as Shane leaned again the rock beside the fissure.

By the moon, he wore nothing but damn jeans again. Seriously, I would have to get some of his shirts from his closet and leave them here, so he could put them on, because staring at his glorious, naked chest was killing me. Even with the scars, he was exquisite.

At least like this, I could stare without shame.

There was no denying he was one of the finest wolf shifters out there. Tall and wide, with thick arms and thousands of smooth muscles, a face with sharp lines that seemed to have been cut by the gods of beauty and envy, his warm brown eyes, and the dark brown hair that curled behind his nape.

It was a freaking shame we didn't belong together.

I shook my head. What the hell was I thinking? It didn't matter if we belonged together or not. Shane had always been a jerk and I wouldn't give him the satisfaction of having me drooling over him.

"Raika," he said, his voice as sharp as his beautiful face. "I know you're here."

"How?" I asked, knowing that he would be able to pinpoint my location now.

Shane turned his face in my direction. "Your scent."

Shit, for a moment, I forgot Shane's sense of smell was even better than mine, especially because he wasn't wearing shackles around his wrists.

He pushed away from the rock and walked toward me as the tingling sensation inside me started again. In a few seconds, the potion's effect was gone, and I was visible again.

Shane halted three feet from me. "What were you doing?"

I shrugged. "What do you mean?"

"You were staring at me." One corner of his lips curled up. "Enjoying the view?"

I scoffed. "You'll never change, will you? You'll always be a conceited jerk." I was supposed to trust this man to save us all? What the hell was I thinking?

"If only you knew," he snarled.

I took a step closer to him and raised my chin. "Knew what?"

He held my gaze, but ultimately, he shook his head. "We don't have time to argue. You can say whatever you want to me, but wait until after we free the pack."

I frowned at him, crossing my arms. "You asked me to meet you here."

He nodded. "Two of my friends arrived last night, Killian and Lavinia. They are both vampires, though Lavinia was a witch before turning and she retained all of her magic. They are outside the barrier, assessing it."

"Assessing it?"

"Lavinia is trying to find out if she, or maybe a group of witches, can bring the barrier down."

"Because with the barrier, they can't come in to help you take Conri down."

"Exactly."

I bit my lower lip, thinking. Shane's gaze shifted to my lips for two seconds before returning to my eyes, the gleam in his eyes darker than before. "Hm, I was wondering ... you don't have a concrete plan yet, right, but you want to invade the pack lands to fight Conri and his demons, right?"

"Right."

"What if we could coordinate things, and this witch friend of yours found a way for me to break the shackles? I could break everyone's shackles and we could attack from the inside at the same time you came from the outside."

Shane's eyebrows curled down. "You think everyone would join the fight?"

"Well, everyone is rusty, but I know everyone wants out. Even if not all of them fight, the others will at least be able to get out of the way."

Shane nodded. I could see the wheels in his mind turning. "That's an idea. When I do come up with a plan, I'll take that into consideration and let you know."

I frowned. So much like a bossy alpha and he wasn't even one yet. Which made me think ... would he let me go once he became alpha? His father wouldn't allow my family and me to move away. He hated us, but instead of letting us disappear from his sight, he kept us close—as an example.

But Shane was my mate. He might not ever love me, but he could at least let me go, for the sake of the bond, right?

"You just came to tell me your friends are outside looking over the barrier?"

His jaw worked overtime. "I also wanted to make sure you're okay."

The always-there tug of the bond flowered in my chest and got stronger. Shane shouldn't care about me. I didn't want him to. It made everything so much harder.

"Please, don't—"

"How's Minsi doing?" he asked, cutting me off. "And Tyren, and everyone else?"

I frowned and quickly told him about them all—Minsi was still the same and I honestly didn't see her improving without serious treatment, Tyren was still a teenager locked in a classroom with six wolves, and everyone else ... I didn't even know. I couldn't think too much about it. It hurt too much to know the Nightshade wolves had stayed seated in classroom corners for the most part of their days for over a year now.

"That's no way of living," I muttered.

Shane let out a long sigh. "We're working on it. Soon, everyone will be free again. And—" He stilled and looked to the side. I opened my mouth to ask him what happened, but then I heard it too. Footsteps coming this way.

With a snarl, Shane grabbed my wrist and rushed toward the fissure. He pushed me inside and followed. We scooted in as far as we could go, but there wasn't much space.

In fact, before I could register anything, Shane and I were in the same position from when the mating bond first snapped. My breasts squeezed against his hard chest, my fingers splayed across his shoulders, his warm skin under my palms. My legs straddled one of his thick thighs, his hands closed around my hips, his fingers touching my exposed midriff, and my ass and back dug into the rough rock behind me.

My face was right at his neck and it was impossible not to smell his alluring scent—a mix of mint and musk and a hint of sweat. It teased my nostrils and filled my mind.

My mate.

The words came unbound to my mind and warmed my body.

Holy moon, this was too much.

Shane lifted one of his hands, brushing my hair aside, his fingertips grazing my jaw and neck as he exposed my skin. A shiver ran down my spine. He looked at me, his breath washing over my face, but we were in the near dark and it was impossible to read his expression—but I felt the tightness of his body, I heard his labored breath, his fast heartbeat under my hand.

Shane lowered his head toward my neck, and touched his nose to my skin. I sucked in a sharp breath and whimpered. He inhaled deeply, his hands digging into my waist once more.

"You smell delicious," he whispered, his voice low.

"Y-you know this is just the bond playing with our heads," I said. But when my body felt so alive pressed against his, it was hard to believe that.

"Do you think this is playing?" He grazed his nose over my neck and moved his leg, pressing it against the apex of my thighs. I bit down on my lip before a moan escaped my throat.

Dear moon.

Shane brushed his lips across my jaw, and I melted in a gooey puddle. I held on to his strong shoulders before I fainted from the sensations sparking to life inside of me. Torturously slowly, Shane brought his lips to mine—

And he stilled again. He snapped his head toward the entrance of the fissure. The footsteps grew louder. A patrol was outside the rock formation.

Shane plastered himself over me, shielding me.

My mind knew we were in danger, but my body didn't care. All it felt, all it wanted was the other body pressed against it. I let my hands move, touching the hard planes of his shoulders, upper arms, and chest. My lust lessened when I felt the scars marring his skin.

I frowned. Seeing the scars and touching them were vastly different.

I glanced up. Shane had relaxed a little, and I realized the footsteps were gone.

One corner of his lips curled up. "Enjoying your new toy?"

A sliver of anger flared up and I held on to it with both hands. I slapped his shoulders. "What the hell?" I pushed against him. "If the demon is gone, then let's get out of here."

"Why? I thought you were enjoying yourself?"

Oh, the cockiness in his voice. I pushed him harder and tried moving, but that only made my body rub against his more.

With a small chuckle, Shane finally moved. He turned as much as he could and helped me out, and I couldn't help but notice how he took the brunt of it—he grazed his body against the rocks inside the fissure, while steering me away from them as best as he could.

I frowned. No, I wouldn't read more into this than I should.

Before emerging from the fissure, we listened. No footsteps, just the regular forest sounds.

Once outside, I inhaled a lungful of fresh air and took several steps away from the fissure and from Shane. My brain needed it if I was going to think straight.

Out here, in the bright sunlight, Shane stared at me with hooded eyes, his body tense, his hands clenched.

Sometimes, I thought he was as mad about the bond as I was. He had always hated me, found me disgusting because I was the pack's omega, and now he was tied to me for life? The stare he gave me now, it was clearly a mix of both lust and anger.

He was ready to pounce on me. The question was: to kiss me or to kill me?

I took another step back.

I didn't know what to say to him, what to do.

Shane saved me the trouble. "My friends are waiting for me. I should go."

I nodded and hugged myself. "Sure."

Fishing something from his pocket, he approached me, a predator stalking his prey. I held my ground. He opened his hand and showed me a small vial. "So you can go back without being seen. The potion doesn't last long, so wait until you're a little closer to drink it."

I snatched the vial from his hand. "Thanks."

He stood there for another moment, his eyes darkening. "I'll be back soon."

And then he disappeared into the trees.

16

SHANE

It was getting harder and harder to leave Raika behind. Several times, I almost went back to her, told her the truth about my feelings, and kissed her. I knew she was as attracted to me as I was to her, but she only knew the jerk, and that was so far from the truth.

I was grieving the death of my parents. Despite everything, my father had cared enough and my mother had been the most caring mother a person could have. But at the same time, I felt free. Even freer than when I was living at DuMoir Castle and pretending I was fine on the inside.

Now, I could be who I wanted to be.

I would take my damn pack back, show Raika the wolf I could be, and we would start over. The entire pack would have a second chance.

I found Lavinia and Killian where I had left them at the disguised tree line before a clearing, where the barrier was. Lavinia was seated right in front of the barrier, her hands touching it, while Killian leaned against a tree behind her, his foot on the tree, his arms crossed, a knot between his brows, his eyes on Lavinia.

I approached him, but Lavinia was lost to whatever spell she was doing. "How is it going?"

"She has been quiet for a long time," he said, his gaze unflinching. "She's still trying to figure out the barrier's make up, if she or others could break it."

To be honest, I didn't like the idea of breaking the barrier. It would expose my lands to anyone. Hopefully, if we broke it, we would be able to redo the spell later.

We watched Lavinia in silence. I kept my senses open, in case of approaching patrols, but my mind wandered to Raika, Minsi, and Tyren. Of course, I cared about the entire pack, but these three were at the top, first and foremost in my mind the entire time.

Soon, I wouldn't be just thinking about them. I would be living with them again, and this time, I would be alpha. Things would be different. It would be better.

A sudden thought popped in my mind.

"I had in my mind that the crystals' magic is what powers the paradise inside the barrier, but what if they power the barrier too? What if the alpha can't command the barrier without the crystals?"

Killian looked at me. "Then if we found the crystals, we could control the barrier."

"The problem will be how to deactivate the barrier using the crystals without disrupting the lands inside," I mused.

Lavinia pushed up from the ground and turned to us. "Crystals are a witch's best friend. If you find one of them and bring it to me, I can find a way to use it to break the barrier." Her brows furrowed. "Maybe, with a crystal, I could make a hole in the barrier so we could get in. Maybe we won't need to take it down."

There were a lot of maybes and ifs, but once more, it was better than nothing.

"But you said you don't know where the crystals are hidden," Killian reminded me.

"I don't know, but since I can cross the barrier, I can search for them."

"Your pack lands seem gigantic," Lavinia said. "Would you even know where to start?"

"According to Raika, Conri has been searching for the crystals since he took over the pack. He must have left sites upturned and clues I can follow. I'll go by process of elimination first."

"You're going to start now?" Killian asked.

I nodded.

"We'll go to the inn." Lavinia slipped her hand into Killian's. "I'll contact the witches, try to find out if someone knows which coven helped your pack and gifted you the crystals. Maybe if we find the right coven, someone knows where the crystals were hidden."

"Or they can break the barrier, since they were the ones who put it up," Killian added.

Lavinia nodded. "That too."

Those were good ideas and gave us more directions to follow, more clues to gather, and if they worked, they would all lead to the same outcome.

I glanced up to the tree tops. The sun was setting. The demons might not have such great hearing and sense of smell as wolves, but I was sure most of them had great night vision.

It didn't matter. I had to do this.

"I'll meet you later at the inn." I stepped through the barrier.

———

THE FIRST HOUR of my search was uneventful. As soon as I crossed the barrier, I shifted into my wolf form—my senses were heightened then, and I moved faster.

So far, I had found several sites where Conri and his demons had dug into the ground and made a mess. Of course, once they were done searching, they didn't bother to clean up.

Most sites were on the perimeter of the pack lands, close to the barrier. But there were others—behind my house, along the streets deep in town, in backyards ... they didn't seem to know where to look for the crystal, so they were digging randomly.

As I went from site to site and tried taking stock of how Conri was doing this, and also figure out why he was after the crystals, I tried remembering the things my father told me when he was in lesson mode—that was the only time when he was more patient and caring. To me, it had always showed me he cared more about the alpha's bloodline and continuing our pack and power, than his own son.

Regardless, I had paid attention to it all because I had wanted to be alpha. I had promised myself, and my mother, that I would be a better alpha than he was.

That dream had died when the pack was attacked and I thought everyone had perished.

But my desire was now back. I didn't want to be the alpha for power alone. I wanted it because it was the only way to help my pack, to free them.

When he told me about the witches and their gifts, my father said nothing was random when it came to magic. What I understood from that was that the crystals weren't in random places. Wherever they were, it had been planned. It was on purpose, to maximize the spell.

But where could that be?

I walked down Main Street, and when possible, close to the square. I even took a peek at the school. The sun had set, and the school was as dark as the rest of the town. If I didn't know better, I would have said the school was deserted.

Like the rest of town.

During my exploration, I found out something else: there were more demons here than I first thought. It turned out the demons had occupied the houses on one side street, three blocks from the main square, and right beside the burnt section of town. I didn't get close, afraid they would see me, but I saw them coming and going, changing patrol shifts, and inside the houses through the windows.

There were at least a hundred demons here.

My friends and I were strong, but I wasn't sure we were strong enough to take on a hundred demons, even with some of the Ironfang pack joining us.

An hour later, I stopped wandering the town, thinking about where the crystals could be hidden. Lavinia could help since she was still a witch and thought like one.

Still in my wolf form, I made my way out of the barrier.

And skidded to a stop as a demon emerged from behind the trees—outside the barrier.

Eyes wide, the human-looking demon stared at me in frozen stupor for a second. I didn't think he had seen me coming through the barrier, but I couldn't be sure.

He reached for the radio attached to the waist of his pants

and clicked on it. "There's a wolf shifter outside the barrier and—"

I lunged at him.

The demon let go of the radio and stepped aside. My claw grazed his shoulders. When I landed and turned to him again, my breath stilled. The demon transformed. The boring-looking human turned into a figure at least a head taller than me with dark-gray skin, a hairless head, pure-black eyes, and sharp teeth in a wide mouth. His clothes stretched but didn't give.

The demon bared his teeth at me. "You think you can take me, wolf?" he teased me, his voice deeper and rougher than before.

Oh, yeah, I could take him. I had to—otherwise everything that had happened so far would be in vain.

I feinted to the right, as if I would make such a rookie mistake. The demon reacted and stepped to the left and I barreled into him, taking him to the ground. The demon moved his big arms at me, pushing me away, and I bit down inches from his face. The demon kneed me in the stomach, but I held my ground. I would bite off his arms, then I would rip his throat out!

From beside the radio at his waist, the demon unsheathed a small knife and jerked it at me. He grazed my ribs with it, and I yelped and jumped away before he was able to sink the knife in my gut.

The demon shot to his feet and held the knife between us.

"Not so tough now," he said, pushing the knife forward.

I retreated a few steps back and looked around. I snarled at the demon before sprinting toward the trees.

The demon turned as I darted past him and opened his arms wide. "You're running from me? Coward!"

I would show him who was a coward.

As expected, the demon walked forward, after me, as if he didn't believe I was really fleeing.

I had fled once in my life—when I had been rescued from the witches and hadn't come directly here to make sure my pack was really gone. I had run away from the pain, from the grief.

I would never flee from anything in my life again.

I gained speed with my run and jumped into the middle of a tree trunk. I used my momentum to scurry halfway up the tree. Then I turned, used a branch for leverage, and jumped right on top of the demon.

He fell back on the hard ground, the knife clattered from his hand, and I bit down on his neck before he could do anything else.

I ripped his throat out.

My chest heaving, I retreated from the dead demon. I stared at him for a second, my anger and adrenaline rearing back, then dashed toward the inn.

As I ran, I couldn't stop the panic from rising. Shit, the demon had been able to radio the others before I had killed him. Conri would know someone was in the area.

Things had gotten exponentially harder.

17

RAIKA

I STEPPED OUT OF MY BEDROOM AND INSTANTLY REALIZED something was wrong. Dixon and Phell were at the end of the corridor, but there were two other demons on the other side, on the second set of stairs.

I frowned, wondering what to do. Should I wake up Minsi and go about our day normally, or should I find out what was wrong before waking her up—potentially upsetting her and triggering a panic attack.

There was no choice here.

Using the back stairs, I walked past the two demons and went down to the kitchen. Once more, I found a lot more demons than before. What was going on?

I opened my mouth to ask what the problem was when Conri walked into the kitchen, his hands inside his pants pockets, his posture upright, his gaze on my face, his eyes serious.

Something was really wrong.

My stomach tightened. Had they found Shane?

I swallowed my fear and faced the devil. "Is everything okay?"

He stalked to me, his eyes never leaving my face. I walked around the island and reached for a mug, as if I was preparing my breakfast and not putting more distance and obstacles between him and me.

Conri stopped on the other side of the island. "Last night, one of my men reported seeing a wolf shifter outside the barrier."

My stomach dropped. "What?"

"He was able to warn us about it before being killed." Conri leaned over the island. "I was wondering if you know anything about it?"

I gasped. "What do you mean?"

"Don't play dumb, Raika. Do you know who the wolf shifter is? Are you helping anyone?"

"Of course not! How would I know anything when we're locked in here? You control the barrier. We can't get out and no one can get in."

"True enough," he said, his voice even. "But that doesn't change the fact that there was a wolf shifter sniffing around the barrier and he killed one of my men."

I pretended to think about it for a minute. "How are you sure it was a wolf shifter and not a random wolf?"

"Because there aren't random wolves roaming this area. Besides, my man would have known."

Usually, wolf shifters were a lot bigger than normal wolves, especially Shane, who was a male and alpha heir. I hadn't seen him in his wolf form for a long time now, but he had always been big.

I grasped for the next ridiculous suggestion. "Are you in good standing with the other packs in the area?" I had overheard Conri talking to his demons about that too. The other packs hated him, and he even considered attacking them. "Maybe one of them is feeling threatened by you."

He pursed his lips. "And what would you feel if it was the other packs? Would you be hopeful?"

I turned my back to him and grabbed the milk carton from the fridge. Taking my time, I came back to the island and poured the milk in the mug. "You want me to lie to your face or your back?"

Conri slapped the counter with so much force, the stone cracked. The mug and the milk carton fell to the floor and I stepped back, my heart racing.

"Is this amusing to you?" he asked with a snarl. "Let me tell you something, little wolf. If another pack comes after us, I'll have them annihilated before they can even think about it." He rounded the island and stood right in front of me. I stood my ground, even though my insides were a buzz of energy and my flight instinct screamed at me. "And if you so much as think about helping the other packs, someone inside this pack, or anyone else at all, I'll kill you." He loomed over me. "But I'll kill Minsi first, slowly and painfully, and I'll make you watch."

My eyes widened.

A grin stretched over Conri's lips. "Now that we have an understanding, I have some matters to attend to." He glanced at the demons in the kitchen. "As you can see, you'll have new friends following you around. Be good or we'll have to continue this talk later."

He winked at me and left.

My knees wobbled, but I locked them and stood upright. I wouldn't break down in front of these demons. I took in long breaths and calmed my heart, but the desperation inside me solidified.

A wolf shifter, a demon dead outside the barrier.

It could only have been Shane. By the moon, was he okay? He had killed the demon, so I hoped he was, but what if he had been hurt?

He had mentioned his friends were around. If Shane was hurt, they would take care of him. Shane was okay. He had to be.

But what would happen to us now? If Conri knew someone was watching, if he increased security, how would we save our pack?

WITH MORE DEMONS not only following us around, but also stationed along Main Street and around the square, it was hard to go on with our day. Minsi was jittery by the time we arrived at the library. I walked in with her, made sure there were no demons inside—and no Shane—and calmed her down before leaving. After making sure the demons wouldn't go in and bother her, I went to the school where I met Rue in the kitchen. There were a lot more demons here too.

Where had Conri got so many demons?

While serving chicken pot pie to each plate, Rue finally asked, "What is going on? Why the extra demons?"

I glanced at Phell and the other five demons at the door. Who cared if I told Rue the truth? I didn't think they would do anything about that.

"One of the demons was found dead outside the barrier last evening," I told her. "Apparently, they think a wolf shifter did it."

Rue's hand froze and she stared at me with round eyes. "A wolf shifter? Outside the barrier?"

"I told Conri it was probably a regular wolf, but he doesn't think so." Wouldn't it have been a lot easier if he had?

"But ..." She glanced at the demons and lowered her voice. "Who could it be?"

I shrugged. It was better if she didn't know about Shane yet. "I have no idea." I wanted to say that I hoped it was someone from another pack trying to save us, but the demons were sure to tell Conri I said that, and if they did, Conri might increase security around me even more.

I was already feeling suffocated as it was.

Not to mention hopeless. How would I talk to Shane now?

"Do you think it's someone who wants to help us?" she asked, her voice even lower.

I met her eyes. If I told Rue, she wouldn't tell anyone else. In fact, she would even help us, but it was risky. Even if the demons didn't have the same hearing as we did, they still could hear our conversation, and that would get us in a lot of trouble. If Conri found out Rue was involved, he would punish her.

I couldn't do that to her. At least not yet, not until Shane's plan was ready to be executed.

"I don't know," I muttered, lowering my gaze.

We continued working in silence, but when we took the food to the other wolves, the silence was gone. The pack members were agitated and curious.

"What's going on?"

"Why are there more demons watching us?"

"I saw more demons in the square too."

"Will they kill us?"

"They will use us for sacrifices!"

Rue glanced at me as we started serving our people, but we didn't say anything. The sentence "I don't know" was my best friend right now.

But Lucille and Dom weren't having it.

When I passed along the plates to their classroom, they leaned against the door.

"You know what's going on," Lucille whispered. It wasn't a question. I looked at her, but neither confirmed nor denied it. "Can't you tell us?"

"Not yet," I whispered back.

Her eyes widened. Dom frowned. "Whatever you're doing, if it means our freedom, we're in."

Lucille nodded.

A sliver of warmth wrapped around my chest. Though these two had practically terrorized me my entire life, they had changed, and right now, they looked at me with a hope that choked me.

"It might take time," I continued. "Don't say or do anything for now."

Dom nodded, but I could see in his demeanor how hope was already changing him.

Lucille's lips curled in a small smile. "You aren't so bad after all."

I scoffed at that. "I was never bad. You were."

"That's what you say," she teased. But then she grew serious and lowered her voice again. "You can count on us."

I nodded, turning my back on them before the demons came to see why it was taking so long.

The questions, the comments continued even after Rue and I left the corridor and went back to the kitchen to clean up.

Now that I was away from them, I worried I had precipitated things by giving a hint to Lucille and Dom. But this thing had been bursting inside of me. I couldn't tell Minsi, and I wouldn't tell Rue yet. I tried remembering Lucille had been in love with Shane for as long as I remembered, and Dom had been Shane's best friend. They would be upset with us if we left them out.

Despite the increased security, I couldn't help but hope when I entered the library to check on Minsi. The girl had ditched her lessons and was sprawled on the rug in the middle of the library, her stomach on the floor, her feet up and crossed at the ankles, and her shoulders propped up by her elbows. If she heard me come in, she didn't say anything.

An invisible hand squeezed my chest. We all needed this nightmare to be over, but Minsi would benefit more than anyone. The girl needed treatment for her panic attacks; she needed real help.

After making sure she was okay, I went to the drawer where I had found Shane's note before, but didn't see anything. I searched between the shelves, under the rug's corners ... there was nothing.

With the increased security, Shane wouldn't be able to come in.

And I wouldn't be able to meet him, even if he called for me.

My chest sank a little.

Whatever plan he was coming up with, I hoped he could act on it from the outside of the barrier, because it seemed we couldn't help him from inside here anymore.

18

SHANE

I paced inside my bedroom, my mind at full speed.

After killing the demon outside the barrier, I decided it was best to hide at the inn for a while. If I stayed away from the pack long enough, things would blow over and Conri would lower his guard again.

I hoped.

The first day was torture. The second was even worse.

At least I wasn't taskless. Killian and I reported to Drake. He said he would let us handle this problem, and when (not if) we needed reinforcements, all we had to do was ask.

Lavinia contacted several witch covens and asked if they knew about my pack's magic. She didn't say anything about the crystals. If Conri was after them, other people could learn about them and come for them too. I already had too much on my plate. Unfortunately, no one knew anything. Some witch covens hadn't even heard of my pack before.

However, Lavinia had talked to Thea and her aunt Almae —they thought that with enough of their witches, they could make at least a hole in the barrier to let us pass.

So now we potentially had a way in and numbers to attack.

But I didn't want to go charging in head-on and risk having Conri kill my wolves out of spite before we even got near the town. I sat down, closed my eyes, and thought through several possible plans.

All my ideas were crappy and way too risky.

Besides, my mind kept coming back to the crystals.

What did Conri want with them? Had he come to my pack for them? Why? There was something about these crystals, and I had to find out what it was, even if it was after capturing Conri and torturing it out of him.

A knock came from the door and I turned to it—and the side of my stomach pulled at me. I hissed as pain spread through my midsection. That damn demon had swept his knife across my ribs. It hadn't been deep enough to make too much damage, but it had been nasty and it hurt like a bitch. Lavinia had applied a healing salve to it, and it finally looked better. But sometimes, depending on my movement, I still felt it.

With a groan, I opened the door and let Killian and Lavinia enter my room with our lunch.

"Seen anyone?" I asked. They knew what I was talking about. Because of the demon's death, Conri could be sending more out and farther from the pack lands, looking for the killer.

I had fucked things up badly.

Killian handed me my lunch and shook his head. "No one unusual." Both of them were also being careful and only leaving their room to grab meals, but each time they did, they kept their eyes and ears open.

I sat down on one corner of my bed, while Killian sat on

another. Lavinia took the chair by the desk again. Deep in thoughts, we unwrapped our food and dug in.

"Shane, I hate bothering you about this again, but the full moon is approaching," Lavinia reminded me. As if I could forget that. "We should attack before that."

"Or after," Killian suggested. Lavinia nodded.

I didn't want to wait until the full moon was over, but I didn't think I had any choice in the matter. The full moon would be at its peak in less than four days. Would we be able to assemble everyone, break the barrier, and clean up the pack lands before that?

It was cutting too close.

I bit down on my burger, chewed, swallowed. "I think we have to wait until after."

Killian nodded. "If we're staying here, we need to find a place to lock you up."

Shit, there was that too. "Right. We'll figure that out. Meanwhile, let's put the plan into action. In six days, after the full moon is gone. Lavinia, call Thea and the others. Ask them to come and help you with the barrier. Killian, call Drake and ask him to send as many vampires as he can spare. I'll contact the Ironfang pack and let him know we're ready."

"And what's the plan?" Killian asked.

There wasn't one, really. "We break the barrier and push in. We spread out and try to surround the town. Then we close in together, pushing everyone to the main square." I frowned. "Lavinia, do you have anything to break the cuffs?" Lavinia and Killian had worn those cuffs when they had been captured by the Nightmist witches.

"I can try to make a potion to melt the metal," she said. "I can add something to neutralize the magic in them, and both should do the trick. I have most of the supplies in my bedroom." She never went anywhere without a bag full of her potion-making supplies. "The rest should be easy to find."

"How long do you need?"

"A few hours at most. It should be ready by tomorrow."

I nodded and ate the last bit of my burger. "Good. Then I'll warn Raika. She'll prepare the wolves and help them with their cuffs." I stood up and threw the remainders of my lunch in the trashcan beside the desk.

"You're going there right now?" Killian asked. "They are probably on high alert after what happened."

Lavinia looked at me. "He knows, but she's his mate." She winked at Killian. "You would have done the same."

"True," Killian muttered. "Just ... be careful, man. Last thing we need is to have you captured."

I nodded and reached for the small pouch on the night-stand—Lavinia had given me more potions after the attack, in case I found myself in trouble again.

"See you later," I said, as I walked to the door. Once outside, I pushed with all my might and ran toward my pack.

Toward Raika.

THE QUANTITY of demons roaming the pack lands had increased tenfold, and if it weren't for Lavinia's potions, I wouldn't have lasted ten minutes in here.

Taking full advantage of the invisibility potion, I circled the house, but only found Minsi in the kitchen with Rue, the old English teacher, and several other demons who were watching over them.

Where was Raika?

Apprehension had its nasty claws deep in my chest while I trekked toward the library—my next stop.

I knew I had made the right choice when I saw three demons standing by the front door. I went around the back, where more patrols wandered the grounds, but no one stood guard.

I shifted back into my human form, put on my jeans, and shoved the pouch in my back pocket. When all the patrols seemed to be looking away, I opened the back door, slipped in, and closed it again.

With silent steps, I crossed the back room and entered the main library, where Raika was. My nostrils flared as her scent filled the air around me, and my heart sped up when I set my eyes on her.

Raika stood by a table in front of a tall pile of books. She opened the first page of a book, looked at something, scribbled something down on the notepad, then put that book away, and did the same thing with the next book.

When she moved one of the books, her pen rolled down and she crouched to pick it up. When she stood back up, she flipped her long dark hair over her shoulder, and lust coursed through me.

She was beautiful. I had always known that, but dear moon, why did she have to wear such short shorts that barely covered her tight ass, and those fishnets over her long, lean legs, and cropped tops that showed off her flat stomach and tiny waist? Was she purposefully trying to provoke me? Provoke any male who set eyes on her?

The tingling of the potion wearing off ran across my skin.

Raika's head snapped toward me and her blue eyes rounded. "Shane," she whispered, and I swear, it almost sounded like she was relieved to see me. She forgot about the books and walked toward me. "How did you—?" Her eyes lowered to the healing wound on my side. She stopped right in front of me, her fingertips hovering over the red lines. "What happened? Are you okay?"

Was that worry? By the moon, I hoped it was. "You should have seen the other guy," I joked.

She frowned, lowering her hand. "I know. Conri told me one of his demons was killed. It was you, wasn't it?"

I nodded, not proud of my actions. But since being taken last year, I had killed more supernaturals than I dared to count. I had turned into a killer, even if a well-intentioned one.

"I had to," I confessed. "He was radioing the others, telling them about me."

"I understand," she said, almost too quickly. "Conri asked if I knew anything about it, if I was helping anyone."

I clenched my fists. "Did he hurt you?"

Raika shook her head. "No. I don't think he knows what's going on, but he's not taking any chances." She gestured to the door. "You probably saw the number of demons crowding the town now, right?"

"I did."

"So, what do we do now? Have you come up with a plan?"

"I did, but first, I wanted to see if I could find some old books in here." I turned around in a circle, eyeing the shelves lining the walls and crowding the space.

"You? Books? Why?"

I sighed and turned back to her. "I think I know what Conri is searching for." I told her about the first alpha, the witches, the creation of our pack, the crystals ... "I don't know where the crystals are hidden, but I was wondering, maybe some of these books have something about it."

Raika's brows lifted. "The pack's recordings."

"Exactly." It hadn't been my intention to come here for the records. I just wanted to see her again, but now this sounded like a good excuse. "My father showed me them when I was younger, but I haven't studied them." Yet. Someday, if it all worked out, I would become alpha, and then I would read them all. "I don't know how far back they are dated."

"We can find out." Raika took the lead. She stopped at the front counter, from where she got a set of heavy bronze keys, then she weaved through the bookshelves to the farthest wall, where the shelves had doors. With the bronze key, Raika unlocked a section and opened the doors wide open. A heavy leather-bound ledger stared back at us. "These should be the town's records."

Dates were written on the ledgers' spine. I counted down, until I found the first one—from almost eight hundred years ago. That wasn't far back enough, but I still picked it up and flipped it open. A fancy handwriting covered the pages and skimmed through the first part. Like I thought, this was the first record from our pack, but it came when the pack was already two hundred years old.

"It's not here." I returned the book back to its place. "Could there be more? Maybe somewhere else?"

Raika skimmed the spine of the records. "I don't know. If there are more, they aren't here. Maybe they're hidden." She would know better than anyone else since she had spent a lot of time in here, and later, this had become her workplace.

"Maybe." I frowned as she continued looking at the spines. "What are you doing?"

Raika picked up the last ledger on the entire shelf. "I thought I could see something." She sat on the floor, folded her legs, and placed the heavy book over her legs. "I'm not sure it would be recorded, but I have to check."

I crouched beside her. "Check what?"

She glanced at me. "Why my family was demoted. Why we became the pack's omega."

Shit. I knew why and I also knew she wouldn't find it there. My father hadn't wanted anyone to find out about one of his lowest points, so he didn't write it down.

"Raika," I started, not really sure what I should say. "Does it really matter? It's not like you can change the past."

She glared at me. "It matters to me." She flipped the pages of the ledger until she found the correct year, but several pages were blank there. Incredulous, she flipped back and forth between the pages. "What the hell?"

"I'm sorry," I whispered.

"You knew it wouldn't be here?" She pushed the ledger to the side and shot up to her feet.

I rose with her. "Raika ..."

"You know, don't you? Why your father did that to my grandparents. To my mother. To me." She stilled. "Tell me."

I shook my head. "It doesn't matter."

She took a step back. "Didn't you hear me? It matters to me."

"But it's not important."

"You're not going to tell me," she whispered. Nodding, she turned and marched between two shelves. "I knew I shouldn't trust you. You're just here to make sure your siblings are okay. You don't care about anyone else. That's okay." She continued mumbling nonsense and weaving through the many shelves as I followed. "We'll find a way."

She abruptly halted and scanned the books in front of her.

"Find a way for what?"

"I don't know why I didn't think of this before. I guess I didn't need it because you had abandoned us. But you're back now, and you'll take over once we defeat Conri. It'll be easier if it's gone."

"Raika, what the hell are you talking about?"

She picked a book from the shelf and flipped it open. "Breaking the bond."

I blinked. "What?"

She traced her finger over the book's contents page. "There are books about magic spells and curses and stuff like that here. I bet one has something about breaking mating bonds." She put the book back onto the shelf and picked up another. "And even if we can't find anything in these books, I'm sure we can find it somewhere. Once the pack is free, I can look for it." I grabbed her wrist and turned her toward me. The book fell from Raika's hand. "Hey!"

"You want to break the bond?" I asked, a snarl in my words. I couldn't help it, but this subject made me angry.

Brows knotted, Raika pulled her hand free from my grip. "It's what both of us want."

"Who says I want to break the bond?"

She stared at me, her eyes wide. "Why wouldn't you? You hate me."

Dear moon ...

In a flash, I splayed one hand on Raika's lower back, pulling her to me, gripped behind her neck with my other hand, and closed my mouth around hers. At first, Raika froze, but when I moved my lips across hers, she whimpered and moved with me. She even parted her lips, letting me slip my tongue inside. By the moon ... her soft lips, her delicious taste, her intoxicating scent, and her tight body pressed against mine.

It was too much and still not enough.

Deepening the kiss, I spun us around and pressed Raika's back against a tall bookshelf. She whimpered again as her hands snaked up and hooked around my shoulders. Her nails dug into my skin and it was pure pain mixed with pleasure.

It was perfection.

I had imagined kissing Raika thousands of times, but none had been this good, this amazing. Her body molded into mine, and her lips seemed to have been made to fit mine.

She was my mate.

She was *mine.*

My body came alive at the thought. Desire flooded every inch of my veins and my pants were suddenly tight.

I broke the kiss, dragged my lips across her cheek at the same time that I slid my hands down her back and around her hips, holding her tight against me so she could feel how much I wanted her.

I whispered in her ear, "Do you still think I hate you? That I want to break the bond?"

Raika stilled in my arms. She put her hands on my chest and pushed me hard. A growl rose in my throat, but I stepped back, giving her the space that she wanted.

"This—" She gestured between us. "—was the bond. Nothing else."

I frowned. "What the hell does that mean?"

Of course that was the bond, but it was so much more. We belonged together and she knew that. Why was she fighting it?

"I don't have to explain myself to you." Raika shook her head and smoothed her hands down her hair. "At any rate, I have to go. Minsi has been with Rue for a long time now. They're waiting for the books." She glanced at me, her eyes hard. "When you have something to share with me about the plan, or what I have to do, you know where to find me."

With sure steps, Raika stepped around me. I wanted to go after her, to hold her arm, to make her talk to me, but I didn't want to push it and have her distance herself from me even more.

So I watched as Raika picked up a handful of books from the pile and raced out of the library, leaving me alone with a massive hard-on.

19

RAIKA

I RAN OUT OF THE LIBRARY AS IF IT WAS ON FIRE.

And it had been. If not the building, then my body while I was so close to Shane.

By the moon, that kiss. As I walked faster than usual toward the house, I tried reeling in my raw emotions and my expression before the demons following me sensed anything amiss, but it was hard.

I could still feel his hands on my body, holding me tight to him, his bare chest pressed against mine, his hips grinding against mine, his mouth moving with mine in perfect synchrony.

A moan rose to my throat and I swallowed it.

Dear moon, what had Shane done to me? Why was he playing with the bond like this? I knew this was the bond, it had to be. There was no other explanation for the way he made me feel.

Right?

I shook my head, trying to get rid of those thoughts, of the exquisite sensations still running underneath my skin, of his scent still flooding my nostrils.

By the moon ...

In need of a cold shower, I marched into the house and stopped dead in my tracks.

Conri was in the family room with two women.

Two witches.

My blood turned into ice.

"Raika." Conri turned to me with one of his demon-like smiles. "I'm so glad you're here. Do you remember Keeva and Lorie? From the Nightmist coven?"

Of course I remembered them. They had been here for Minsi's birthday party. The two of them along with a handful of witches had run the show that night since the coven princess and her right hand hadn't come. They had been the ones who kidnapped Minsi and threatened her life if Shane's father didn't do what they wanted.

And they were here, right now, under the same roof as Minsi.

A wave of rage and despair flooded my veins. I glanced around, but didn't see Minsi anywhere. Hopefully, she had been in her bedroom the entire time and didn't know these witches were here.

"What are they doing here?" I asked through gritted teeth.

"Raika, behave, little wolf." Conri walked toward me. He reached for my arm, but I jerked it out of reach. "They are visiting us. After all, it has been almost a year since they last visited."

The night of the attack.

The night these witches captured Shane and kept him from us.

My insides thrummed with built-up rage. I almost acted

on it on impulse. I imagined myself shifting into my wolf and ripping their hearts out. It would have been a quick death, and they didn't deserve that.

"I remember you," Lorie said. She had brilliant red curls, and she smoked a long and thin pipe. "The omega. Aren't you a pretty one?"

"Indeed, very pretty." Keeva narrowed her eyes at Conri. Her blond hair was tied in a loose bun at the base of her neck. Both witches wore gowns that belonged to the ball-room. "Why do you have the omega in your house, Conri?"

Good question.

"Never mind that." Conri's smile lost a little of its shine. "Just ... leave her alone." I stared at him. Did I hear a hint of threat in his voice?

Keeva winked at him, probably imagining what everyone did—that I was his damn pet and he did with me what he wanted.

In his damn dreams.

"You're making us curious," Lorie said. She looked me up and down. "We love curious things."

Conri ignored the witches. He turned to me, his grin back. "Lorie and Keeva are here to help me with something," he said. "Be nice to them, and helpful. Mostly, stay out of their way. They will be coming and going often from now on."

I wanted to scream. I wanted to kill them right here, right now. But what could a shackled wolf do against two powerful witches and a half-wolf, half-demon?

"Can I go now?" I asked.

Conri stepped aside and swept his arm wide, letting me pass.

I ran up the stairs and went to Minsi's bedroom. I opened

the door slowly, afraid of scaring her, but I shouldn't have bothered.

Seated on her bed and rocking back and forth, Minsi was out of it. Lost to a deep panic attack. It had probably started with screaming, but now it had turned within.

Rue sat by her side and ran her hand up and down Minsi's back. She lifted her tearful eyes. "There was nothing I could do. Once the witches entered the house, she lost it."

My heart wilted.

Slowly, I approached Minsi. "Hey, pretty girl," I called her, my voice soft. I sat on Minsi's other side and glanced back at Rue. "Did they do anything to her?"

"They teased her, which I think only made things worse. I dragged her out of there as fast as I could, but she was so out of it, she fought me too. After a while, her energy waned, and she became like this."

I cursed under my breath. I should have been here, if I had, maybe I could have lessened the blow, made this panic attack a little less intense. The way Minsi looked now, trembling and mumbling under her breath ... this had probably been her worst attack to date. I leaned against the headboard and pulled Minsi with me. I cradled her in my arms, holding her tight.

"It's okay," I said, feeling ridiculous for lying, but what else could I say to her? "It'll be okay. I'm here now. I'll protect you." And soon her brother would come too and he would save her.

Save us all.

We just had to endure a little while longer.

RUE LEFT in the middle of the night, after Minsi finally relaxed enough to sleep. The demons took her back to the school, where they would lock her in her classroom.

I stayed in Minsi's bedroom all night, holding her close in her twin bed. I dozed off here and there, but I couldn't relax, not when Minsi had had such a terrible panic attack and there were Nightmist witches inside the house.

Were they staying here? Conri mentioned they would be coming and going often. I hoped not. In fact, I had to talk to him. I would beg to not let them come in here again, for Minsi's sake. I knew he didn't care, but for some reason, sometimes he relented to some of my wishes, the ones that didn't seem to affect his plans.

I hoped this was one of those.

In the middle of the morning, I dragged myself from Minsi's bed. Relieved she seemed to be in a deep, peaceful sleep, I went to my bedroom where I took a quick shower and changed into clean clothes. Soon, it would be time to go to the school to help Rue make everyone's lunch, but I wasn't so confident about leaving Minsi alone.

If only Conri would allow someone else to help Rue, so I could stay with Minsi.

No, that would be two requests too many. I had to choose the most urgent one and forget the other.

But for now, I had to do only one thing: breakfast for Minsi and me. She would wake up soon, and if I could feed her before she had another panic attack, then I would consider that a victory.

With Phell and another demon following me, I went down through the back stairs to the kitchen. I looked around, but the house seemed empty, except for the demons, Minsi, and me.

Feeling a little lighter, I grabbed eggs, bacon, bread, and started on our breakfast. It didn't take but three minutes for my mood to spoil.

The house's front door opened and Keeva and Lorie walked in.

I braced against the broken island countertop as I glared at them.

"Good morning," Keeva said in a sing-song voice as she strolled into the kitchen wearing a big smile. Today, she wore a deep red gown.

Lorie sniffed the air as she joined us. "Hm, it smells delicious." She leaned over the island and grinned at me. "But not as delicious as you."

I frowned. "What's that supposed to mean?" I raised a hand. "You know what? Don't tell me. I don't want to know. Just leave me alone. In fact, why don't you just leave? There are plenty of empty houses in town. Pick one." I turned my back to them and went back to the cooktop, where my scrambled eggs were starting to burn. Shit. I turned off the stove.

Keeva and Lorie approached me, one on either side of me.

"I don't think she knows," Lorie said to Keeva.

Keeva leaned closer, almost over me. "I think you're right."

By the moon ...

With the frying pan and my almost-burnt eggs, I went back to the island, and placed the eggs in two plates.

The two witches followed me.

"Aren't you curious?" Lorie asked me. "It doesn't matter. We'll tell you either way."

"We can sense something different about you, little wolf," Keeva said, sounding proud of herself.

I frowned at her. Only Conri called me that and I hated it. And now they were spewing lies to aggravate me.

They were succeeding.

"See, we don't know what exactly, but I remember seeing you during the little girl's birthday. You were hiding beside the infirmary building." I sucked in a sharp breath. She had seen me there. "I sensed it back then."

Keeva nodded. "True, a handful of us sensed it. The most powerful ones, of course." She winked at me. "But you see, other problems arose and we forgot about that."

"Until you came in last night." Lorie's eyes sparked with excitement. "Maybe that was why your family was demoted to omega?"

Say what? That got my attention, and I checked on the bacon while the two followed me wherever I turned.

"No." Keeva shook a long index finger right at my face. "From what I heard, her family was demoted to omega long before she was born."

"Oh, so maybe Franc didn't know," Lorie mused.

"No, not Franc, but Conri sure knows."

"And that's probably why he keeps you close."

I stilled. The spatula in my hand snapped in two. "Stop spewing nonsense!"

Lorie's eyes bulged, but she smiled wide. "You don't believe us. Ask Conri. You know, we will ask him about it."

"We're very curious." Keeva pointed her finger to my chest. "There's something here. Like a faint, deep but ancient kind of magic. Something I had never encountered before."

"Me neither." Lorie picked up one of the bacon pieces from my plate and took a big bite of it. "Curious."

"Interesting," Keeva said.

Lorie nodded. "That too."

Holy moon, I wouldn't get this breakfast done. I would either grab a knife and slice their throats open, or I would throw the rest of this food over their heads. Either way, I would get in trouble and I was damn tired of that.

Pretending I wasn't curious at all, I turned away from them. Breakfast be damned. I would starve if they continued in this house. Hopefully, they would leave and I would be able to cook. If not for me, then for Minsi. The girl had to eat.

I took two steps before Keeva wrapped her hand around my wrists, just above the shackles, and tugged me back to them. "Where do you think you're going? We're not done with you."

I shoved her away from me, but froze when Lorie grabbed my chin in her hands, her long nails pressing against my skin. Her other hand was up and a sliver of black smoke swirled around her index finger.

Magic.

"I would behave, if I were you." Lorie moved that finger closer to my chest. "If you don't want to feel any pain."

"What are you doing?" I asked, trying to sound brave, but failing. "Why don't you leave me alone?"

"We're very friendly," Keeva told me. "We love welcoming new witches into our coven, and we also love making friends. We thought you would want to be our friend too."

"Especially because if we dig in, we can find out about the magic we're sensing." Lorie touched her finger to my chest. "Don't you want to know what it is? What it means?"

Keeva clapped her hands twice. "We do."

"You're insane," I rasped, moving my chin as little as I could. Lorie's nails dug in a little more.

"What in the name of the underworld are you two doing?"

In half a second, Lorie and Keeva took their hands off me and faced an angry, red-faced Conri.

"Oh, we were just playing with your toy," Lorie said. The magic around her finger was gone. "Isn't that what you do with her?"

Conri's arms shifted. His fingers elongated, turning into claws, and dark-gray fur covered his arms and shoulders. He glared at the demons standing watch at the corners of the kitchen.

"What the hell were you doing? Why didn't you stop this nonsense?"

Phell let out a scoff. "She didn't seem to be in any real danger, sir."

Conri growled, showing off his half-turned fangs.

Boy, he was pissed.

He stalked to us. He glanced at the witches. "You don't touch Raika, or the other girl, without my consent. Do you understand? If you do, our deal is over."

The witches exchanged an I-told-you-so look, but nodded at him.

"You're no fun, Conri," Keeva complained.

"You're not here to have fun," he snapped. His fangs retracted, and slowly, the fur disappeared from his arms. "You're here to work." He pointed to the front door across the family room and the foyer. "Now go."

The witches shot me an amused glance before flipping their hair and walking to the door like models on a runaway.

Once they were gone, Conri stared at Phell and said, "If the witches try anything else, you stop them. If you can't stop them, call me. No one is to hurt Raika."

"Yes, sir."

Finally, Conri looked at me and let out a long breath. "Are

you hurt?" I shook my head. "Good." He gestured to the plates and food at the counter in front of me. "You can return to whatever you were doing."

Without another glance at me, Conri walked away, taking most of his demons with him, except for Phell and the new one who had been assigned to me.

I stared at Conri's back. Could Lorie and Keeva be right? Was there something different about me and that was why Conri kept me close, keeping me safe? Was that why he seemed concerned about me?

But it didn't make sense.

Because there wasn't anything different with me. I would have known if there was, right?

No, I wouldn't allow the witches to play with me like this. They didn't deserve my fear, my curiosity.

Taking a deep, calming breath and shaking those thoughts out of my head, I threw the cold food in the trash and started it all over. Despite my mood and my sudden lack of appetite, Minsi deserved a good breakfast.

20

RAIKA

I HAD SEEN SHANE THE DAY BEFORE—WHEN WE KISSED IN THE library—but when night fell and I found myself alone in my bedroom, it felt like an eternity had passed.

After the witches' game in the morning, the rest of the day went by almost normal. Minsi had woken up feeling better. She ate all of her breakfast, but asked to stay in her bedroom the rest of the day. She promised she would do all of her lessons, but safely in here. As much as I hated for her to stay cooped up inside for several days in a row, how could I drag her out knowing Lorie and Keeva were roaming around the pack lands?

Besides, today was the attack's anniversary. She was probably thinking of her parents and everyone else who had perished that night. I knew I was.

I stayed with her for as long as could, then I went to the school. Rue noticed I was quieter than usual; she asked me about it.

"Is it because today marks one year?"

I nodded. That and a lot of other things.

When we took the food to the pack, everyone was quieter and gloomier than usual. All of them knew what day today was.

Even Lucille wasn't jabbing at me as usual.

"I know there isn't much I can do for you from here, but ... hang in there," she whispered to me before I left.

Odd how things were. If a year ago someone told me Lucille would be saying kind words to me, I would have laughed so hard. What a joke.

But it wasn't a joke.

Rue insisted she could handle cleaning the kitchen and prepping for tomorrow. "Just go home and take care of Minsi."

I didn't like leaving her to do it all by herself, but I was worried about Minsi, so I didn't argue.

The rest of the afternoon crawled by. In her bedroom, Minsi worked on math and Spanish lessons, while I skimmed the crime book I had started several days ago. After all that had happened, I wasn't in the mood to read about violence and suspense anymore.

Thankfully, no one else came to the house the rest of the day. When I went downstairs to make dinner, a demon informed me Conri had lit a bonfire in the main square and he and the witches were having a party to celebrate his reign. He would return home late.

I hoped the witches didn't return at all.

Almost back to her usual self, Minsi went to bed early. I stayed with her until she fell asleep, then I went to my bedroom. I turned on one of the lamps flanking my bed and stared out the window, my eyes shifting from the trees to the stars in the sky. I couldn't see the moon from here, but I knew it would soon be a full moon. Those were almost painful. Wolves had a special connection with the moon, especially when it was full, but with these damn shackles, there was nothing we could do.

I stared at the trees, as if Shane could magically appear from among them.

I would be relieved if only I could get a glimpse of him from a distance.

"What are you looking at?"

I yelped and turned around, eyes wide, hands out in defense.

And saw nothing.

A moment later, the air seemed to shimmer right before my eyes.

The invisibility potion wore off and Shane appeared two feet from me, wearing only jeans again.

"What the hell?" I asked, my voice low. "How ...?" I glanced to the closed door then drew the curtains behind me. "How did you get in?"

"I slipped in earlier, when you were in Minsi's bedroom," he told me, a mischievous grin on his lips.

"And you have been watching for the last, what, five minutes? Creep!"

His grin widened. "What can I do? You're beautiful. It's hard not to stare."

I rolled my eyes at him. I walked past him and locked my bedroom's door. I wasn't sure if it would help to muffle our voices, but I grabbed a towel from the bathroom and shoved it against the bottom of the door.

"You shouldn't be here."

He placed a hand over his heart. "And I thought you would be happy to see me."

"Idiot. I am happy, but—" I saw the small duffel bag on my bed. "What is that?"

Shane opened the bag and fished a couple of glass vials from inside. "Potions."

He explained to me what they did and about his plan. I would pass these along to the wolves at the school and once we heard the signal in about six days, we would use the potions on our shackles to melt them. We would be free and be able to attack from the inside, as I had suggested.

Hope bloomed in my chest. Now that was a plan and I liked it! But that hope dwindled once I remembered the new faces around town.

With a frown, I stashed the bag under my bed. "So six days until we act? Why so long?"

Shane averted his eyes. "It's the time my friends and allies need to get here."

"Did you come directly here? You haven't been in town?"

He shook his head. "I came directly here."

"Then you don't know."

I told him about seeing Lorie and Keeva in the house this morning. Shane's body stiffened and his nostrils flared. I didn't tell him what they said about me, because I didn't think they were serious, and even if they were, it didn't matter. But I told him Lorie had grabbed my chin. I even lifted my chin and showed him where her nails had scratched my skin.

Shane's eyes darkened, his hands curled into fists. He marched toward the door.

I stepped in front of him. "What are you doing?"

"They hurt you. I'm going to kill them." He was serious. If I hadn't stepped in his way, he would have gone after the witches. "And I'll kill Conri too. The moon knows he deserves it more than anyone for all he did to you. To Minsi."

"That's suicide." I rested my hands on his bare shoulders —and instantly regretted it, but I didn't pull away. "You can't help us if you're dead. Live to fight another day, isn't that the saying?"

The faint light from the lamp illuminated half of his face and cast longer shadows on the other side, making the angles of his jaw and chin sharper, his eyes brighter, and his mouth plumper.

"Think about Minsi," I added. "Think about Tyren. They need you." I paused, knowing all too well these words would doom me, but I didn't care. "I need you."

Shane's eyes softened. "I thought you hated me."

"I do." When we were younger and he had been mean to me, I did. When he had learned about the bond and hadn't done anything about it. We had had days from Minsi's birthday to the attack and he hid it from his father, from everyone. And when I thought he had abandoned us.

But now I knew the truth about that. He hadn't abandoned us and the proof was right before my eyes. Hadn't he risked his life so many times coming in the pack lands while it was swarming with demons to check on us? On me? "Probably not as much as you hate me, though."

"Raika ..." He paused. "Go to my bedroom. The bottom drawer of my dresser, under my old sweaters, you'll find a thin shirt box. Bring it here."

I stared at him. "Why?"

"Just bring it here. Please."

Frowning, I shooed him to my bathroom and closed the door before I stepped out my bedroom. Phell, Dixon, and two other demons stood guard at the end of the corridor, several feet from my door. They didn't even look at me as I walked into Shane's bedroom, as if I did that every day.

I found the white shirt box where he told me. I picked it up and walked out of his bedroom holding my breath, but again the demons didn't even look in my direction. I slipped into my bedroom, locked the door, and placed the towel against it once more.

Shane walked out of the bathroom. "Open it."

Curious, I sat down on my bed and opened the box.

I gasped, looking at all the things that lay inside.

An old pink hair tie, a broken silver pen, a paper I had written for history class about why wars were stupid and what everyone could do to avoid them, a library card, a picture of me and my grandparents when I was a little girl, another picture of Minsi and me seated on the library's center rug, laughing our heads off.

I picked up a crystal button that had fallen from my favorite leather jacket a couple of years ago. "I wondered where this had gone. I searched for it. I wanted to sew it back on."

"I saw it on the library's floor right after you left," he said. "Sorry."

I put the button back in the box. "You know this makes you look like a bigger creep, right?"

He nodded. "But it was the only way for me to have something of you. To feel closer to you."

I frowned. "Why?"

"Because ..." He sat on the bed on the other side of the open box. "You ensnared me in your web the first moment I saw you. I don't know, it might have been the bond already pulling me toward you, but I like to think it wasn't. That I was a goner because you were you." He gestured toward all of me.

My heart squeezed. "But ... you were mean to me."

"Give me examples."

I thought for a second. "Once after math class, I forgot my jacket in the classroom. You picked it up and came after me. You snapped at me in the corridor when you shoved it to me, saying I shouldn't leave my filthy stuff behind."

He shook his head. "When you left your jacket there, I saw that as an opportunity to get close to you, to look into your pretty blue eyes without anyone's judgment. I snapped at you, yes, because everyone was watching. But I didn't say filthy. I believe that was Lucille. Or Mace."

"There was once when I was leaving the library and someone walked fast by me. I don't remember who. He bumped hard into my shoulder and I fell on my butt. There were plenty of people around and they all laughed at me, saying I was clumsy and ridiculous, just what they expected from the omega. You were there. You stomped to me and stood over me, yelling at me to watch out where I was going so I didn't hurt anyone."

"I didn't yell, but I said it firmly. And then I helped you up."

"What?" I blinked. "No, you—" I swallowed my words as I remembered more of that day. Yes, he helped me up. "You did."

"I snapped at you because everyone was watching, but I helped you up and made sure you weren't hurt. Besides, it was a way for me to hold your hand."

"My first day of school," I continued, remembering another one. "I was alone at a table in the cafeteria and everyone was bullying me. You came to me and ordered me to leave. Lucille said something about being too disgusting to eat in the same room as me."

"I sent you away to protect you. I thought it would be better for you to eat in a classroom than to have the bullies harass you. I wanted to do more but couldn't."

This was crazy.

"Then what about the time you picked up Minsi from the library, saw us together, and snapped at me that I was too old to be her friend." In a way that was true. I was nine years older than her, but Minsi had always been shy and reserved. She didn't get along with any other children. She found solace in books, and as a bookworm, we had bonded over them.

"That was when I took this picture." He pointed to the picture in the box. "I did that when Dom and Mace weren't looking. I snapped at you because they were with me. I had to maintain appearances."

Damn it, he was twisting my memories. "And why did you have to maintain appearances? Because you couldn't be seen fraternizing with the omega?"

"In a way, yes." Shane ran a hand through his hair. "You know my father demoted your family. I didn't know the reason yet, but he hated your family so much, no one could utter any of your names in his presence. How could I tell him that I liked you, that I wished he would give you a chance to prove yourselves? You know as well as I do, he wasn't a nice man. He led the pack well, he was almost always fair, he cared about the well-being of the pack as a whole, but he was a jerk and lost his temper too often."

I wondered ... "Was he a jerk to you too?"

Shane nodded. "I think he expected too much of me because I was his heir. He was nicer to Tyren and Minsi. And he was great with my mother. Whenever she was around, it was like he flipped a switch and became pure mush for his mate."

"Your mother was nice," I said. "I didn't have much contact with her, but when I was with Minsi at the library, she always treated me with respect and kindness."

"I think she noticed how I felt about you," he said, and his words still caught me by surprise. Here he was confessing his long-standing feelings for me, but I was still having a hard time swallowing the truth. "Once, when she saw I was having trouble accepting the way my father wanted me to be, she told me to hang in there. She said I could pretend to be like him for a while, and then once I became alpha, I could change everything. I could be a kinder alpha; I could undo what had been done to your family. You have to understand, I was young. I was so afraid of disappointing my father. Besides, every time I did, I had to face the consequences."

"He hit you?" I posed it as a question, but I already knew the truth.

"Sometimes, when I veered too far away from his vision. But I kept in mind what my mother said. One day, I would be alpha and I could be better than he was. A lot better. But for the moment, I had to endure it."

My heart squeezed. "I never knew," I whispered, lost.

I stared at Shane as if seeing him for the first time. He had liked me since we first met in school. He had protected me in the way he could, even when it seemed he was being mean to me. He had talked to his mother about being a better alpha and changing everything, changing things for me.

Shane never hated me.

But ...

I frowned. "What about when the mating bond snapped?

You didn't tell anyone; you didn't do anything about it. Was it because of your father?"

He nodded. "I was afraid that if he knew, he would hurt you and keep you from me. I didn't do anything about it, but I was trying to come up with a solution. How could we tell everyone and keep you safe? But before I could figure out—"

"Conri attacked," I finished for him. I was baffled. All these answers ... I hadn't expected this from him. "Why?"

"Why what?"

"Why did you do all of this? Why did you care? You had no reason to. You barely knew me. All you must have seen was an angry girl who lost her temper and retorted, which got her in more trouble."

The corner of his lips tugged up. "I barely knew you. I confess, yes, it began because you were pretty, even as a child, and that made me curious. I thought the omega would be an ugly monster. But you were beautiful. And when I saw you cowering because of the others, I became protective. I didn't know why. Then, with time, I ended up taking notice of everything else. I swear, not in a creepy way. I didn't go out of my way to stalk you, but you were everywhere I looked. Perhaps it was the bond already pulling me toward you."

I shook my head. I had never had much contact with him, but I did see a lot of him. He was the damn alpha heir, and he was always surrounded by other wolves who I thought were trying to kiss his ass. Especially Lucille, Dom, and Mace, three of my worst tormentors.

"It is a little creepy," I joked, trying to lighten the mood.

He shrugged. "I call it being protective. And while I was being protective, I got to know you. Your favorite color is teal, but you wear mostly black. Your favorite food is cheese lasagna followed closely by caramel ice cream. You love music and wanted to take dance lessons, but the dance teacher wouldn't let you join the studio. I know you love reading and could read at least a book day, if you had your way."

"I wish I had the time to read more."

"I know. I also know you are kind and like to be helpful and you have the most beautiful and contagious smile I've ever seen, and you practically only show it to my sister. I know you are smart and had great grades even though no one left you alone in school. You could have acted on your anger so many times, and yes, you snapped here and there, who wouldn't? Honestly, I don't know how you controlled yourself. But that showed me you are strong, brave, and fierce. Even now, with everything stacked against you, without any hope, you went out of your way to make sure my sister is well, that our pack is being taken care of."

My cheeks heated up. "I think you're seeing things." I definitely wasn't all of that. In my mind, I was lonely, insignificant, scared, and weak. He was mistaken.

"No, Raika, you're the one who doesn't see yourself. You're amazing. You're beautiful inside and out." He stared at me, those eyes locked on mine. "I'm so incredibly proud to be your mate."

I sucked in a sharp breath as if I was seeing him for the first time.

He wasn't a cocky bastard. No, that had been a facade so his father wouldn't punish him, or his siblings, for being weak. But he wasn't weak. He put on a brave face, and he endured it all. He protected his siblings, and he protected me.

I had no idea Shane had done all that for me, that he had cared that much, that he had kept his distance from me so I wouldn't be hurt.

My heart squeezed and the bond deep inside my chest warmed up.

"I think I preferred when I thought you hated me," I whispered.

He cocked his head. "Why?"

"Because it was easier to hold on to anger."

Shane pushed the open box to the side and scooted closer to me, his eyes never leaving mine. "What are you feeling now?"

"It's a jumble right now, but I'm not angry at you anymore. And I certainly don't hate you. Far from it."

Shane reached to me and picked up my hand in his. "Do you *don't hate* me enough to let me kiss you right now?"

My throat grew dry. I nodded.

Shane hooked his hands around my hips, pulling me toward him. I fell into his lap, my legs straddling his, and my chest pressed to his. My breath came out in little bursts as one of his hands splayed on the small of my back, pressing me against him, while the other closed around my nape. He brushed his lips on mine, and I practically whimpered.

By the moon.

Who was I kidding? I wanted this. I wanted him.

I wrapped my arms around his shoulders and parted my lips to him, letting him in.

Letting him take all of me.

21

SHANE

RAIKA'S MOUTH ON MINE, HER LEGS AROUND MINE, HER CHEST brushing against mine ... she felt like a fucking dream I never wanted to wake up from.

For years, I had watched her from a distance, but rarely let myself think about her this way, to imagine we had a chance. Especially because I had no idea she was my mate.

But she was. Raika was my mate, and when I found out, I was elated. It had been all I ever wanted ... but my father would have killed her if he had known. That was why I sent her back to town right after we found out and my father found us. I wanted to protect her from him, from everyone.

I told my mother, though, and she had smiled at me, a true smile, and told me she was happy for me. "She'll be what you need," she said to me. "Don't worry, we'll figure something out."

Not knowing what was coming, I held on to that. For five days, I breathed and lived trying to find how I could do her justice, how I could announce to the pack, to the whole damn world, that she was mine and I was hers, and the rest be damned, and still protect her from everyone's wrath.

Then the world exploded and I thought I had lost all of them. When I was locked away in the witches' dungeons, I had begged for death to find me. I had wanted to die and be with Raika in the afterlife.

If only I had known she was alive.

No, I wouldn't think about that now. I wouldn't torture myself with those thoughts, especially not when Raika was right on top of me, her arms around me, and her mouth on mine.

I kissed her with all the pent-up desire I had for her, and by the moon, it was so much. I claimed her mouth as her scent and her desire filled my nostrils.

Dear moon ...

I wrapped an arm around her waist, and without breaking the kiss, swiftly shifted us on the bed. I laid her down on the mattress and lowered myself on top of her. She wrapped her legs around my waist, tugging my ass with the heel of her feet, pulling me closer. I relented, thrusting into her, the layers of our pants doing nothing to hide how much I wanted her.

She gasped against my mouth and it was all I could do not to rip our clothes off and take her right here. I moved again, pressing my hips into hers, and the bed creaked.

We both froze, not even daring to breathe.

I pushed up from the bed slowly and retreated toward the bathroom. If the demons decided to check on Raika, I could hide in there. Not that I wanted to. My will right now was to kill them all on the spot, but I knew that it would complicate things.

But after three tense minutes, no one came.

Raika stood from the bed. She placed her hands on my chest and pushed me back, into the dark bathroom. She closed the door with her foot and locked it with one hand. Only a sliver of moonlight streamed from the tall window above the shower.

"We won't need to be as quiet in here," she said, a naughty gleam in her blue eyes.

By the moon ...

I advanced on her, claiming her mouth again, my hands already at her pants—I wanted them off right now. Raika helped me push her pants down to the floor and when she was free, I closed my hands around her ass, my fingertips touching the lace of her panties. I picked her up, deposited her on the bathroom's counter. She instantly opened her legs, and I stepped between them and glued my body to hers.

Raika ran her hands around my shoulders, down my back, and I couldn't help but shiver at her divine touch.

My mate.

This gorgeous woman was my mate.

I knew fate couldn't have chosen better for me. In fact, I thought fate was too damn good for me. I didn't deserve her.

But I sure would try to.

Her hands slid down to the waist of my pants and she deftly undid the button and zipper. Then she slipped her hand inside and cupped my hard-on. My knees buckled and I almost lost it right there. It had been so long, and even then, next to her, to what she meant to me, to how she made me feel by looking at me, I knew things were about to reach a new level.

I couldn't wait.

Raika moved her hand along my length, bringing fire within me, and my body trembled in pleasure.

"Dear moon," I whispered before dragging my mouth down her neck, tasting her smooth skin.

I grazed my teeth along her collarbone and Raika shivered in my arms. Suddenly, I had a new goal: make Raika shiver in pleasure several times a day.

She continued moving her hand along my hard-on, and my thoughts became jumbled, pleasure taking over, and I wanted to do the same for her.

It pained me, but I grabbed her wrists and pulled her hands back. She stared at me, her eyebrows cocked.

"We'll go back to that later," I told her. I placed her hands on either side of her, her palms flat against the counter, and reached for her panties. Black lace ... should I have expected anything less from a girl who wore short shorts, crop tops, and fishnets?

And she was all mine.

I ripped the side of her panties, rendering them useless, and knelt in front of her.

Raika's eyes rounded.

I touched my lips to the inside of her thigh, and Raika sucked in a sharp breath. I placed a kiss on her soft skin, then dragged my lips higher. Raika's legs tensed, and she started closing them on instinct. I rested my hands on her knees and held them open.

Finally, I brought my mouth to her center and licked her clit. A moan ripped from her throat and her body jerked. I glanced up and found Raika leaned back against the mirror, her eyes half-closed, her mouth open ... so damn sexy. I closed my mouth around her clit and sucked hard. She jerked again. I would have to add that to my list of goals.

Then I played with her. I licked her, grazed my teeth,

sucked, and flicked my tongue over her clit, making her tremble more and more. When I slipped a finger inside her, Raika's hands came to my head and she knotted her fingers in my hair.

I smiled against her center and increased my assault. I slid another finger inside her as far as I could before pumping them in her, fast and hard. Her gasps became more frequent, though she bit down on her lip to muffle them, and her body alternated between trembling and tensing. Knowing she was almost there, I continued thrusting my fingers into her, and I licked her clit, increasing the pressure from my tongue.

With a muffled cry, Raika fell apart. Her entire body quivered as she came. I watched as she rode that high, her eyes closed, her mouth parted—so beautiful, so damn sexy. I kept pumping my fingers in her as I stood. Then I pulled them out and licked them—delicious.

Raika opened her eyes "That was ..." Red stained her cheeks.

"You're so damn beautiful." And so damn sexy. I dipped over her, pressing my mouth to hers, kissing her like I hadn't before—and she kissed me back hard.

Raika tugged at my pants and I started pulling them down—

Then I froze.

Faint voices reached my ears.

"What is it?" Raika asked.

I placed a hand over my lips, unlocked the bathroom door, and spied out the bedroom's window. As I thought ... Conri, Lorie, and Keeva walked down the house's front path, followed by at least a dozen demons.

"Shit," I muttered.

Raika came to my side and looked out the window. "You need to leave. Now."

"I know, I know." I turned to her, wound my arm around her waist, pulled her to me. "I don't want to."

She pushed against my shoulders. "You have to."

I leaned into her, brushing my lips to hers. A soft moan rose to her mouth as she kissed me back. She relaxed in my arms, but then she pushed me back again. "Please, Shane, they can't find you here. They will kill you on the spot if they do."

Not only that. Keeva and Lorie knew about me and the full moon. They had done this to me. If they saw me ... they would tell Conri about it. They could use it against me.

Still, it was damn hard to leave her here.

"Raika, I might not come back until it's time for the attack."

She frowned. "So ... six days."

"Yeah. I need to help my friends in the meantime." I hated lying to her, but it was better if she didn't know about this yet. "It'll go by fast, don't worry."

She scoffed. "I'm not worried." The joking tone of her voice brought a smile to my lips.

I fished the potion from the back pocket of my pants and drank it. I felt the tingling of the potion taking effect immediately and I pressed my lips to Raika once more before I became invisible.

"I'll be back soon," I whispered to her. "I'll send you a signal when we're ready. Please, be careful."

A knot appeared between her brows. "You too."

I paused at the window, not because I was watching for the patrols—though it would be easier if no one saw the window opening and closing by itself—but because my feelings flooded my chest. I wanted to tell her more. I wanted to let Raika know exactly how I felt about her.

But I had to believe we would have time for that later.

Conri and the witches came into the house and I silently slid the window open, climbed out, and left.

But this time, my heart stayed behind.

22

RAIKA

WHEN I WOKE UP THE NEXT DAY, I THOUGHT IT HAD ALL BEEN A crazy dream. A crazy, hot, delicious dream.

Shane in my bedroom, the things he told me, the way he looked at me, the way he touched me.

What we had done in the bathroom.

My cheeks heated up and my body tightened just remembering it.

Yeah, definitely not a dream.

But like a dream, it had been amazing. Shane's hands on my body, his lips on mine, the way he held me, his hot body pressed against mine ... we would have gone all the way, if Conri and the witches hadn't come back to the house.

My body tightened and heat pooled low in my stomach. Shane was sure experienced, but I wasn't. Being the omega in our pack, it wasn't like I had many prospects. No one had looked at me that way before. I hadn't even kissed anyone until Shane, let alone had sex.

And I was freaking twenty years old!

I had used my hands before, though, several times. I had

thought that was good, but Shane had blown that out of the water. What he had done to me—his face buried in the middle of my legs, his tongue lapping over my clit, his fingers inside me—dear moon, that had been amazing. Exquisite. Incredible.

Pushing thoughts of Shane and his hot body aside—there was no way I could get rid of them entirely, and I didn't even want to—I went on with my day. There was a lot to do and I had to get everyone ready before Shane and his allies attacked.

Today, I chose ripped skinny jeans, a belt with the same spikes on the bracelets over my shackles, just to match them, and a fitted black tank top. I put on my black booties, and let my long hair loose down my back. To top it all off, I picked up a large leather jacket from my closet and filled the inside pockets with all the potions Shane had brought last night.

Ready for battle, I commenced my day.

Thankfully, the witches were nowhere to be seen, and I invited Minsi to have breakfast downstairs with me. After breakfast, she got ready and we headed to the library. I loaded her up with lessons, then went to the school a little earlier than usual—I had stuff to do.

When Rue arrived, she smiled at me. "You're early again."

I nodded at her. "Just a tiny bit."

We moved with ease around the kitchen; the demons stationed by the door barely paid attention to us. When Rue halted by my side at the big working table in the middle of the kitchen, our backs to the demons, I slipped a piece of paper and a small glass vial toward her.

Rue's eyes widened, but she didn't miss a beat. She pocketed both the paper and the vial, and went on with her chores. We prepared the food and served the plates. We placed it on the cart and headed to the classrooms where our pack was imprisoned.

The demons watching the door in the middle of the corridor stopped talking to each other when they saw us coming. They stiffened and opened the door for us. One thing had changed after Shane killed the demon outside the barrier: Now Phell and Berth went in with us. The door was locked again from the outside while Phell and Berth leaned against it on the inside.

At the first classroom, Rue passed along the plates while I grabbed one of the papers from my jacket's inner pockets, along with a couple of vials. I let my head fall to the side, using my long hair as a curtain, and passed the papers and vials to Vianna, a widow with two children under ten. The other six children in the pack were in the room with her, and I hoped her motherly instincts kicked in and she took care of all of them when it was time to act.

At the next classroom, I called for Tyren. He ignored me at first, but when Rue used her teacher's voice, he dragged his feet to the door.

"What?" he snapped at me.

"Here." I handed him the paper cup with water, and tucked in my hand were the paper and a couple of vials.

His eyes bugged, but he moved swiftly. He grabbed the cup and hid the rest. "Don't expect thanks," he snapped again, though this time, his gaze was softer.

We moved to the next classroom and I gave the note and potions to Roman, who like the others, quickly hid them. He gave me a slight nod of his head, as if he wanted to tell me he was ready for anything.

Next was Jay, the healer apprentice. With his trembling

hands, he almost dropped the potion and note, but stashed them away and tried to act normally.

Rue and I went on like that from cell to cell, always choosing someone we thought would handle it right, who would read the note explaining everything and hide the potions until it was time.

In the last classroom, I passed it all to Lucille.

She stared at me, just as surprised as the others, though she knew I had been planning something. She didn't know with whom. With a nod, she pocketed everything.

As Rue and I left, a sense of mission accomplished filled me, even though I knew this was just step one of a long list of things that had to go right, or we would fail. But now, our pack was armed with a potion to melt their shackles and the door locks, along with two potions that acted as bombs, which they would use on the demons guarding the corridor. All they had to do now was to wait five days for the signal—it was all written on the notes I had passed along with the potions.

I probably should have waited until it was the last day to hand the potions to them all, but I was afraid that if something went wrong, if something happened to me, or if the signal came sooner than expected, then they wouldn't be able to act.

Rue and I returned to the kitchen and I felt energized. Hopefully, in a couple more days, I wouldn't have to clean this damn kitchen and cook for so many people ever again.

It was all coming together now.

Soon, we would all be free.

23

RAIKA

I TAPPED MY FOOT ON THE FLOOR AND READ THE SAME paragraph again. The letters jumbled in my mind and I couldn't register any of it. With a groan, I pushed the book aside and glanced up.

Across the table, Minsi stared at me, her books and lessons forgotten in between us.

"Everything okay?" I asked.

She nodded. "You're tense."

I gaped at her. She had spoken! And she had stated the obvious. I had come back from the school almost two hours ago and hadn't been able to relax since. I felt like Shane's signal would come at any second now and we had to be ready. I patted my jacket and felt the remaining vial there with enough potion to melt Minsi's and my shackles. I would carry it with me whenever I went now, and preferably, I wouldn't be too far from Minsi when it happened. My priority would be to free her and get her out of here before any real fighting started.

"It's nothing," I told her. It was better if she wasn't aware of anything until it all went down. "Go back to your lesson."

Minsi rolled her eyes, but lowered her head and continued reading.

Impatient, I stood up and walked around, gazing at the books on the shelves. I went to the small selection of fiction titles in the library, hoping something would spark my interest. I really could get lost in a fantastical world right now, but I had read almost everything in here—or at least, everything that looked good to me.

A faint clank sound came from outside. Frowning, I walked to the windows lining the outer library wall and spied out.

Lorie and Keeva stood at one corner of the main square along with a handful of demons. Lorie said something and pointed to a low stone bench that curved with the corners. A demon lifted a sledgehammer above his head and hit the stone bench. The sound came again, stronger this time, and a large piece of the bench's top broke and fell into the street.

What the hell were they doing?

Conri walked nearby, looking around at the main square, as if he was searching for something.

My stomach sank.

The crystals. Had they found them? Was that why Conri had invited Keeva and Lorie here? In some covens, each witch had a different gift. Maybe their gifts could lead them to the crystals.

I shifted my weight, my fingers itching. If only I still had a phone or internet connection. I could call Shane and tell him what was going on.

Shit, if they found the crystals before Shane attacked and we were freed, then I doubted we would ever have a chance like this again. I had to do something. I had to get out of here. I had to warn Shane.

A shout came from across the street. I watched as Conri, the witches, and all the demons turned toward the school. Two demons walked from the school's front door, carrying a shackled Lonan between them.

I frowned. What the hell?

Conri met them halfway. Lorie and Keeva forgot about the bench and went to see what was going on. I bit the inside of my cheeks as I watched. Conri said something, Lonan said something, back and forth they went for a minute, until Lonan was screaming at Conri.

Demons surrounded them, obstructing my view.

Shit.

Another minute passed and Conri pointed toward the library. He yelled something, but I couldn't make out his exact words, just the tone of his voice—and he was angry.

A bang came from the front of the library. My heart squeezed and I ran toward Minsi. Phell and Dixon marched inside and toward us. Minsi shot to her feet, trembling instantly. I pulled her behind me.

"What's going on?" I asked, retreating. The demons kept advancing. "You're not supposed to enter here, remember?"

"Shut up and come with me," Phell said as he grabbed for me. I had had only a few fighting lessons in school, but that didn't stop me from raising my fists and punching Phell. Or trying to. The demon transformed in front of me. His human form gave away to a shimmery dark green skin and a swirl of shadows. His eyes turned black, his hair disappeared, and when he spoke again, his teeth were razor sharp and his tongue forked. "You don't want to fight me."

My shoulders sagged, my arms falling to my sides in surrender.

I had seen him in this form during the night of the attack, the night he had killed my mother. For over a year, he had posed as a perfectly statue-like human. But now, as he brought back his true form, I almost cowered in fear.

Behind me, Minsi screamed and I woke up from my stupor. Regardless of what Phell was, I swung a fist at him, and it would have landed beautifully on his chin, if he hadn't slid to the side, as if he had blinked into the shadows for a second.

He grabbed hold of my arms, and Dixon went for Minsi.

"No! Leave her alone!" I yelled as I jerked against Phell's hold. In this form, he was a lot stronger than me, and with the shackles around my wrists, I had no chance, but desperation filled my veins.

The shadows around Phell suddenly wrapped around my arms. Phell's eyes widened. He swept his hand between us, recalling the shadows.

What the hell had that been?

I didn't have time to process anything, or act again, as Phell tied both my hands behind my back and pushed me out of the library. I called for Minsi, but I lost sight of her once I was outside. I could still hear her screams.

Conri, Keeva, Lorie, Lonan, and a plethora of demons waited for me at the corner of the square, right beside the broken bench. Lonan was like me, his arms behind his back, demons holding him, but he had his chin high and his gaze dripped with venom.

Phell brought me face-to-face with Conri.

I scowled at the devil. "You promised you wouldn't let

your demons go in the library, and now you have me dragged out of there? What's going on?"

Conri stared at me, his face darkening. "I should be the one asking you what's going on." His voice was cold, almost threatening. "Lonan here has an interesting story to tell." He glanced at Lonan.

"I told him about your plot," Lonan said, baring his teeth at me. I froze. "You're helping someone. I don't know who, but I know he'll somehow break through the barrier and attack soon."

My blood went cold. "W-what? That's the most insane thing I have ever heard!"

Lonan scoffed. "She's pretending. You saw the potions."

My heart stopped.

Conri nodded. He lifted his hand and I gaped at the small vial between his thumb and index finger. "These potions." He unscrewed the cap and smelled it. "I wonder what they are for." He passed the vial to Lorie.

She sniffed at it. "Oh, this will melt the metal of the cuffs while neutralizing its magic."

"Interesting." He erased the short distance between us and loomed over me, his arms still shifted. "So you've been helping someone from the outside. That's who killed one of mine, isn't it?"

"I don't know what you're talking about," I said, my voice tight.

He reached for me. He patted my arms, my waist. "Hey!" I shouted, trying to squirm out of his way.

Conri slipped his hand in my jacket's inside pocket and pulled out the vial. "You don't know what I'm talking about?"

I lifted my chin. I wouldn't give him the satisfaction. "No, I don't."

I didn't even see it coming. Conri's fist connected with my stomach and the air fled my lungs. Pain spread fast and deep, and I fell on my knees, my vision darkening. Someone pulled me back up, but my feet were unsteady.

Conri's mouth widened and he showed me his wolf teeth. "I have all the proof I need." He gestured toward one of the demons beside Lonan. His hands were full of vials and notes. "If you deny it, it'll only hurt more."

My eyes widened and rage took over. I glared at Lonan. I had so many questions. Why would the others tell him, knowing he was a pain in the ass? Why would he turn against his pack like this? Against his buddy Serge? What did he have to gain in telling Conri? But all I could say was "What the hell?"

Lonan snickered at me, as if he was the smartest cookie around. "I saw some of the others whispering about something. I asked what they were hiding, but no one told me. But I made sure to quietly move close enough to listen to them. You're waiting on a signal from someone. When that happens, we were supposed to use the potion on our shackles and attack from inside."

I still didn't understand. "Isn't that better than staying in that classroom and rotting away?"

"Not when the help comes from you." He spat on the ground between us. "I would rather die in that cell than have the omega help me with anything."

I shook my head. "What is wrong with you?"

"Nothing. I came to Conri bearing gifts. Now, he'll let me go while you all rot in those cells." His snicker widened. "Or worse."

"What?" I stared at Conri.

"About that." Conri turned to Lonan. In a swift move,

Conri swiped his claw wide. Three gashes appeared on Lonan's neck and blood oozed out. The man gurgled and fell to his knees.

Horror and fear laced my insides, and I took a large step back.

Conri's claws disappeared as he turned to me. "Now that that is taken care of, what shall I do with you?" He narrowed his eyes at me. "I should use you as bait."

I froze.

"We can help with that," Lorie said.

Without looking at them, Conri nodded. Lorie and Keeva strolled to the center of the main square and started moving their hands, doing some kind of spell. All the while, Conri didn't take his eyes from me, and even though I wanted to cower and run, I held my ground and stared back at him.

Three minutes later, Keeva said, "It's done."

Conri nodded and Phell pushed me toward the witches. I jerked against him again, but it was no use. All he did was tighten the ropes around my wrists, and I hissed in pain.

We walked toward a wide black circle on the ground. Oh, shit.

Phell pushed me inside just one step—I felt the rush of the circle's magic brush against me—then he untied the rope from around my wrists before pushing me harder. Arms free, I stumbled to the center of the circle.

I turned and found them watching me—Conri, Lorie, Keeva, Phell, and a dozen demons. In the background, two demons took Lonan's body away.

"You're waiting for someone's signal?" Conri asked, a victorious smile over his lips. "Then wait for it here."

My chest tightened. Shit, this was bad. I looked around—

at the library and at the school. "What will happen to the others? And Minsi?"

"I thought about putting Minsi in with you, but I'll be honest, the girl's screams make me want to kill her myself," Conri said nonchalantly. "For now, I'll take her to Rue."

A relieved breath escaped me. Being locked in the classroom with Rue wasn't ideal, but nothing had ever been. It was still better than leaving her alone at the house with him.

"As for the others ..." He tsked. "When Lonan told the guards what was happening, one of your friends used the potion on her shackles and shifted. She attacked Lonan, but my demons stopped her." My breath caught. Lucille. "She's now unconscious in the classroom used by the healer." He paused. "I'll let that serve as an example for now, but I haven't made up my mind yet. I might punish a few more to be sure they will behave."

I wanted to ask why the hell he needed all these wolves? Why not let them go? But his answer would probably be that it was best to kill them all instead of letting them go.

"No one will come," I lied. "You're wasting your time."

"We'll see about that." He glanced around, as if bored. "Make yourself comfortable. You're staying here until we catch whoever is behind all of this."

He turned his back to me and the first thing I did was to slam my palms against the circle's invisible wall.

Lorie chuckled. "That circle is attuned to you. You're not getting out of there unless we undo it."

Keeva winked at me.

A growl started low in my chest. Damn, how I wished this circle and these shackles were gone. I would rip their hearts out. I had never killed anyone, but I would gladly make an exception for these two.

For all the demons.

For the devil.

I held on to that rage as Lorie and Keeva walked away too. They spoke to Conri for a few minutes. Again, Conri gestured toward the broken bench. When he left, the witches returned to the broken bench.

My rage seeped out of me when Dixon emerged from the library, carrying a sobbing Minsi in his arms. I ran to her, only to slam into the invisible wall and bounce back, almost falling on my butt.

"Minsi!" I called, but the girl was shaking and crying so hard she didn't hear me.

Dixon disappeared with her inside the school and I hoped Conri hadn't lied. That he would allow her to stay with Rue. Rue would know what to do. Minsi would be well.

Would she? Would we?

My legs finally gave out and I fell to my knees. My hands shook; my breath came out in little painful bursts.

Lonan had betrayed his pack because of his hatred for me. And what had he gained from it? Death.

Lucille was hurt because of him, and only the moon knew how she was, if she would recover.

The potions were taken and our plan was gone.

Minsi had been dragged to the school and would probably have a hard time calming down.

The witches were searching for the crystals. Actually, by the way they ordered the demons to start breaking another one of the stone benches in the main square, I was starting to think they had actually found the crystals.

And I was locked in this circle, unable to leave and warn Shane.

Oh, dear moon, Shane ...

I wished he wouldn't come. I wished he wouldn't see what was happening, but I knew he would come at some point, even if it was in a few days, to give me the signal we had been waiting for.

He would see me locked in here.

And he would fall for this trap.

24

SHANE

THE NEXT DAY, I MADE ALL THE NECESSARY ARRANGEMENTS. I asked Lavinia to call on Thea and Almae, and for Killian to have some vampires come too. I sent a message to Ironfang and told them to meet us in five days. By then, everyone should be here and the full moon would be long gone. Hopefully, Lavinia, Thea, and Almae would be able to break through the barrier.

We had also found an abandoned farm a few miles south. Killian bought a shit ton of chains and we would use that during the full moon.

By the moon, how I hated this.

I wanted to see Raika but decided not to go. It was getting riskier to come in and out of the pack lands, and we were close to attacking. It was best if I stayed back for these next five days. Soon, she and the others would be free and I wouldn't have to sneak in to see her anymore.

However, the next day, I was restless. I knew it was because the full moon would start tomorrow and it was already affecting me.

I was also alone. Killian and Lavinia had gone to check if everything was set up at the farmhouse, and then they would bring us dinner.

I paced in my room at the inn. It reminded me of how restless Killian was when Lavinia had been taken by our enemies—I knew how he felt and I wanted to go back in time and stop myself from all the times I had told him everything would be all right.

I didn't want things to be all right *soon*.

I wanted it to be all right *now*.

Caution be damned. I had to see Raika, even if it was from a distance. Even if I remained among the trees at the property's edge and saw her through the house's back windows.

When the sun began setting, I armed myself with Lavinia's invisibility potion, shifted into my wolf, and ran to my pack lands. Once I was close to the barrier, I stopped long enough to drink the potion and then continued running.

I weaved through the trees in the forest and raced to the house.

I frowned when I got closer—it was dark and there were no demons. I focused on my hearing, but there was nothing. No movement, no breathing, no sounds coming from inside the house.

Where could Raika and Minsi be?

My next guess was the library, though at this time of the evening? Weren't they usually at the house by now?

Trying not to jump to conclusions, I made my way to the library. After all, where were two bookworms the happiest? But as I approached the center of town, the atmosphere changed. Demons stood close by or patrolled the streets, making it more difficult for me to sneak closer—but not impossible.

One of the houses on Main Street had an outer staircase that led to the rooftop. I used it to go up, and from there, I jumped from roof to roof, careful with my landing and any loose tiles. I got closer and closer to the library.

At the last building, where a clothing shop had been before, I halted, my eyes on the scene below.

Several of the streetlamps around the main square were turned on, illuminating the dozens of demons stationed around the place.

Across the street, Conri was seated at the diner's outdoor patio, eating his dinner as if he was watching a Broadway show.

In the main square, Lorie and Keeva stood at one corner, throwing spells at the ground, where they had broken a stone bench. In fact, the benches in all four corners had been broken and a dark circular mark stained the ground where they had been.

A memory clicked into place.

"The moon is an important factor for wolf shifters," my father had said when he told me about the crystals. "It's also important to the witches. But you know what else is important to them? Cardinal points."

North, south, east, and west.

Lorie and Keeva had found the crystals in each corner of the square, which were exact cardinal points. But they hadn't been lucky to think about that. No, they relied on magic. I remembered Lorie's gift was sensing magical items. Shit. Though, apparently, they couldn't get to them.

That was troublesome, but it wasn't the worst part.

No. The worst part was right in the center of the stage. Raika, lying on the ground, her hair spilled to the side, her body limp, and a dark witch's circle around her.

Pure red-hot fury filled my veins.

I jumped off the rooftop before I could even think about it.

I ran at the witches. This time, I didn't care if anyone heard me, and some demons did as I ran past them. They searched for the sound's source but didn't find it.

The witches also noticed something was amiss right before I lunged at Lorie's chest and buried my fangs into her throat. She fell, and by the time her body hit the ground, she was dead.

Keeva screamed and threw magic darts randomly. I dodged them all and rammed into her. She fell back as I felt the invisibility potion wearing off. She threw her hands out, trying to push me away, but in physical combat, I was a lot stronger than witches. I clamped my mouth around her neck. She writhed under me for a couple more seconds and then she stopped.

I looked up, and as expected, found all the demons surrounding me.

I couldn't help but steal a glance to the center of the square—Raika was seated, her hands on the ground, her eyes wide, her face pale. She was fine. Being held captive, probably as a trap for me, but she was fine.

A tiny sliver of relief emerged in the middle of my rage, but I pushed it back. I would make the entire world burn down.

I snarled and advanced on the demons.

"Stop!" a voice carried through the square.

I stopped, not because the voice had commanded, but because the demons stepped back and parted, allowing Conri to walk closer.

"Ah, so you're the one behind all of this," Conri said, an

amused grin on his lips. "Welcome home, Shane, former alpha heir."

I shifted into my human form. "I'm still the alpha heir and soon I'll be alpha."

Conri's eyebrows lifted. "Such confidence. It's a shame that's not enough." Conri waved his hands at me.

The demons advanced on me. I barely had time to shift before they were on top of me.

"No!" Raika yelled.

I fought with all I had, clawing the chest of a demon, biting down on another's leg, ramming into another, but there were too many, and their abilities as demons were unexpected.

One sent waves of shadows that obscured my surroundings, while other's breath made me dizzy, and another's scream sapped my energy.

Then, a handful of demons held me by my limbs—and the cuffs were clasped around my front legs. I shifted back into my human form, my strength sapped.

"Shane!" Raika called.

I groaned and pushed to my knees.

A pair of demons held my arms, and another fisted my hair and pulled my head up, so I could look at Conri.

"I'm curious about one thing," Conri started. "The Nightmist witches were supposed to take you, torture you for a bit, and then kill you. How did you escape?"

I stared at him. He wouldn't get an answer from me.

Conri chuckled. "Suit yourself." He glanced at the demons behind me. "Take him to a classroom by himself."

My turn to be amused. "What? Too afraid to kill me?"

"Oh, I will, but I think it would be best to prepare everything for that," he said. "Wouldn't it be something if your entire pack watched your death? Their last hope ... dead. It'll be quite the show."

I jerked against the demons and a couple of them had trouble holding me back. If my energy wasn't shit right now, I would have pushed to my feet and lunged at Conri. With or without shifting, I would kill him.

Conri turned to leave and I assessed the situation. Around me, the benches were broken, and Raika, now on her knees, was in some kind of prison. How long had she been there? For a couple of hours? Since yesterday? I didn't want to think about it.

"I want to make a deal."

Conri stopped. "I don't think you're in any shape to offer me anything."

"What about the crystals?"

"Shane, no!" Raika shouted.

Conri's eyebrows lifted for one brief second. "What do you know about the crystals?"

"I know you're after them. Isn't that why Lorie and Keeva were here? To find and retrieve the crystals for you? And now they are dead."

He stood quiet for a moment. "You know how to access the crystals?"

I nodded—a lie. "I do, and I'll tell you how to do that, on one condition: You let Raika and the others go."

Conri stared at me for a moment. Deep down, I knew he wouldn't agree to that. He had kept them here for so long he wouldn't let them go now.

But he surprised me when he said, "Deal."

25

RAIKA

I KNEW CONRI HAD LIED TO SHANE.

The moment Conri said he agreed to Shane's deal, a dozen demons surrounded Shane and took him to the school. I shouted, banging my fists against the circle's magic. I knelt on the ground, my mind and heart racing.

Holy shit, what had happened? Shane had blown his advantage. He had killed Lorie and Keeva, both witches bleeding out not too far from me, and I had to turn my back to them before I threw up.

Shane had also agreed to show Conri the crystals, but he didn't know anything! Unless he had lied to me.

Would he lie? It didn't matter. What mattered was that Conri wouldn't release us. No, he would probably use us as a dangling carrot to force Shane to obey.

I sat down on the dirty ground. I had been in here for over twenty-four hours. The demons brought me a little food and water, just enough to keep me from starving, and when I needed to use the restroom, the witches had magicked a curtain and a portable potty for me—when I was done, they magicked it away.

I never felt more humiliated in my life—and filthy, tired, and hungry.

Sometime later, Phell and Dixon halted outside the circle.

"Come," said Phell.

I frowned. How was I going to cross the circle? The witches were dead and the circle still held. But most important ... "Why?"

Phell sprinkled some powder on the circle's black line. It shimmered and faded. "Come before it closes again."

Wary, I stepped over the circle's line and was surprised when I walked past the boundary.

Phell and Dixon didn't waste time. They grabbed my arms and dragged me away from the circle. "Where are you taking me?"

"Stop asking questions," Phell said. "It won't change anything."

I opened my mouth to ask again, but took one glance at Phell—at his changing eyes and face—and swallowed my question.

Phell and Dixon took me to the school. They led me down the corridor opposite from where the rest of the pack was, and where a wall of shadows stood. Phell waved his hand and an archway appeared in the middle of the wall.

Beyond it, Conri stood like a king in the middle of the corridor, his eyes on the classroom door in front of him— Shane leaned against the door, his shoulders and head visible through the top glass panel. This side of the school hadn't been modified. There were no bars on the windows and doors, but I was sure they were just as strong.

His eyes widened. "What is she doing here? You said you were going to let her go."

"Oh, I will," Conri said. "I'll let her and the others go, after I have the crystals in my hands."

"That's not what we agreed." Shane slapped the door.

Conri shrugged. He didn't even look in my direction as Phell and Dixon pushed me into the classroom across the corridor from Shane's. The classroom had been emptied of everything—there were no desks, no chairs, no shelves, no school materials. There was only a thin mattress and an even thinner blanket on the corner.

They locked the door and I stood behind it, watching Shane through the glass panel. There was so much I wanted to say, so much I wanted to tell him, but I wouldn't open my mouth while Conri was here.

Instead, my eyes brimmed with tears at the desperation etched in his features.

"You lying snake," Shane snarled.

"I'm half demon," Conri said, proud of himself. "I'm not called the devil for nothing."

"Let. Her. Go."

Conri took a step forward, standing right at Shane's door. His height grew another foot and shadows surrounded him. "I don't think you're in a position to make demands, boy."

Shane didn't flinch or avert his glare from the devil. "I'm going to take everything you have," Shane said, his voice low and tight.

With an amused chuckle, Conri returned to normal. "Oh, this is fun. Unfortunately, I don't have time for this. How about you tell me how to access the crystals now?"

Shane's jaw worked. "The chambers where the crystals are locked have a key." So he did know how to get to them?

He told me he didn't. "Last I heard, my father kept the key in his office in the town hall across from the main square."

"I know where it is," Conri snapped. "I've been there before. I didn't see any key in there."

"It's because it's hidden. You know the portrait behind his desk? There's a vault behind it."

"A vault? How to do you open it?"

"The key to the vault should be in the last drawer in his desk, along the back, probably taped to the bottom of the drawer above it."

Conri glanced at me and I fought an urge to step back, even though the classroom door was between us. He returned his gaze to Shane. "Okay. We'll try that. But if you're lying ..." Conri turned toward the shadow wall then paused and glanced at the demons. "Bring him some clothes. I don't want to keep staring at him naked."

Phell and the other demons nodded as the shadow wall parted for Conri. He walked out, the demons with him, and the wall closed once more.

I stared at Shane through the two doors and glass separating us. "Are you insane? You're going to let him have the crystals?"

Shane shook his head. "Of course not. I lied to him. I have no idea how to get to the crystals."

"But ... he's going to come back and he'll be *mad*."

Shane shrugged. "I can take it." He splayed his hands on the sides of the door. "More importantly, how are you? What happened?"

I let out a sigh and told him about Lonan's betrayal because he couldn't swallow being helped by me, the damn omega. "I knew he hated me, he never hid that, and I think he hated me even more after our capture, but I had no idea he could do something like this." I had really thought he would put up with me for a little longer for the pack's sake.

"That's insane," Shane whispered.

"Alas, Conri loved it. He killed Lonan anyway, and put me in that witch's circle as bait." My brow furrowed. "And you fell for it. Why? You shouldn't have done that. Now our plan is ruined. You're stuck here with us, and your friends are stuck outside the barrier. There's nothing we can do now." And it was all my fault. If I hadn't been caught, if I had waited to distribute the potions, if I hadn't trusted the entire pack ...

"Raika," Shane started. His eyes darkened. "When I saw you ..." He shook his head once. "I knew I was walking into a trap, but I didn't care. I had to make sure you were okay."

My heart squeezed and the pull of the mating bond drew me toward him. Damn, how I wished these doors were gone. "I'm okay, but again, we're all stuck in here. I don't know what we can do now." I didn't tell him about how Minsi had been dragged to the school by Dixon, and she was probably still freaking out. That would only make him more distressed. I was glad we couldn't hear her screams from here.

"My friends will realize what happened and they will act."

He explained that Killian and Lavinia had been out, but they would soon get back to their inn and realize something was wrong. They had friends on the way. The witches would work on breaking the barrier, and Ironfang would rescue us.

If they could bring the barrier down.

I frowned, not liking our odds. "So, what do we do now?"

"We buy ourselves time. That's why I sent Conri on a wild goose chase over a key that doesn't exist. When he comes back, he'll let out his frustration on me, but I can take it."

My frown deepened. I didn't like that idea. "What will you do then?"

"I'll send him on another fake chase. Conri won't be able to help it. If he wants the crystals, he'll have to check it out. We'll be buying my friends the time they need to break through the barrier."

I nodded, though I hated the idea of Shane being tortured. I hoped his friends figured out he was gone fast, and that the witches were powerful enough to break through the barrier in no time.

Because the way things were going, I didn't see any other way out of here.

AT SOME POINT, Shane and I tired of standing in front of the doors to see each other. We both sat down on the floor and talked here and there. We didn't receive any food or water, though Phell had brought Shane some sweatpants and a shirt. As night fell, the exhaustion accumulating in my bones took over. I scooted to the mattress in the corner and lay down, my hands folded under my head. In a matter of seconds, I was asleep.

But my sleep was restless and full of nightmares.

I only saw a jumble of images, and they were more horrible than the others. Conri had put Shane in the witch's circle and used his shadow magic to whip Shane's back, drawing blood and screams. With each crack of the whip, Shane grew weaker and smaller, his wounds opened more and more, and blood was everywhere ... until Shane disappeared and all that was left was a giant red pool.

I saw Minsi screaming and clawing the walls of the classroom she was being held, her nails broken, her fingertips raw and bleeding. When she looked at me, her eyes were feral and her teeth were razor sharp, like the demons'.

I saw Phell in his demon form, not just killing my mother in front of me, but holding her limp body while he buried his jaw in her chest and ate her flesh, her heart.

I woke up with a start in the near darkness. Only a sliver of moonlight coming from the windows bathed the room. At first, I thought the nightmares had been real. But when I heard rapid footfalls and grumbles from the corridor, I knew that was what had woken me.

I shot up and looked out from the small window atop the door. Conri stood in front of Shane's door, along with six demons.

He banged on Shane's door. "Wake up, scum!"

Shane appeared on other side of the door. "Can I help you?"

Shadows swirled around Conri's legs. "You lied to me. There was no key in your father's office, not for the vault, nor for the crystals, but you knew that. Perhaps there's no key at all."

Shane frowned. "No, there's a key. If it's not in his office, then maybe at my house? Maybe in his nightstand?"

The shadows around Conri's legs grew and took over most of his body. "There is no key, is there? You thought you could play with me. Because the worst I could do was torture you. You're wrong."

A demon turned and reached for my door. He unlocked the door and stepped in. Fear flooding my veins, I retreated.

"What are you doing?" Shane pounded on his door. "Leave her alone! Your problem is with me."

"But I won't get anywhere with you if I don't use her. Or maybe your sister. Which one will it be?"

Two more demons entered the classroom and I backed away to the farthest wall. When they advanced toward me, I didn't let them take me. I settled my feet apart, bent my knees, and brought my fists up. I even landed a pretty punch to one demon's chin before the other two grabbed my arms and tied my hands behind my back.

I screamed and kicked my legs up, choosing anger instead of the immense fear inside me.

The demons dragged me to the corridor and threw me in front of Conri. I fell on my side, my hips bumping the hard floor, pain spreading down my bones. I groaned, but didn't give them the pleasure of screaming.

Shane punched the door. It rattled violently. "Let her go!"

Conri crouched beside me. "Little wolf, here we are again." He grabbed my chin and made me look at him. "This will be fun." He stood and opened his arms wide.

The shadows around him shot forward, curling around my legs. Panic surged forward, and I kicked at it, trying to get away, but suddenly, I wasn't in control anymore. The shadows pushed me to my feet, and curled around my torso and arms.

I glanced at Shane and the desperation in his eyes matched the way I felt inside.

The shadows tightened, squeezing my muscles until I gasped for air that wouldn't come.

"Stop!" Shane punched the door again. "Stop this right now!"

The shadows didn't stop, and the pressure increased. My vision darkened, my head lolled forward ... I was going to faint.

But I didn't. Just as I was starting to blackout, the shadows eased and I fell on the floor like a sack of potatoes. I inhaled deeply and coughed, my lungs burning in the process. My arms and legs felt heavy, the agonizing pain blinding me. I wanted to cry, but even that seemed impossible right now.

Conri kicked me in the stomach, and I curled into a ball, fighting the knife-like pain across my ribs.

"STOP!" Shane roared. He hit the door again so hard that I swore it would break.

Conri pressed a hand to the door and shadows spread over it. When Shane struck the door again, a shock jolted him back.

"I'm in charge here, boy." Conri gestured toward me. "As you can see. If you know how to get to the crystals, you will tell me, and you will tell me the truth, otherwise ..." He toed my shoulder and I scooted back, even though moving hurt too much. "This little wolf will suffer more and more with each of your lies."

Shane's eyes turned deadly and his jaw clenched so hard, I thought he would break his teeth. "Fine," he finally said. "I know what to do, but there are two pieces to it."

"Tell me."

"I have to do it. The magic around the crystals is tuned to my bloodline."

"The alpha heir."

"Exactly."

"What's the other thing?"

"The full moon. I can only activate the magic during the full moon."

"The full moon is tomorrow," Conri stated.

I pushed up on my elbows, dragging myself to a seated position. I wondered what Shane's game was now. Was this another one of his lies? Or was he still trying to buy time for his friends?

Shane nodded. "I know."

Conri tilted his head, considering it. "All right. We'll wait until tomorrow evening. But be warned ..." He stepped right to Shane's door and stared into his eyes. "If this doesn't work, I'll kill Raika slowly and I'll make you watch. Then, I'll do the same with your sister." A wicked smile spread over Conri's lips. "I'll do that to your entire pack, until no one is left. By then, you'll be begging me to kill you, and you know what I'll do? I'll keep as my prisoner, alone, powerless, so you can always remember what you did to your pack."

Shane stared back at Conri, serious and deadly. "I'm not lying."

"Good." Conri turned. He paused, looked down at me, waved his hand at me as if I was litter in his path. His demons grabbed my arms and dragged me inside the classroom again. They dropped me just beyond the door before locking it behind me. "I'll be back tomorrow evening," Conri said from the corridor.

I heard their footsteps retreating and then silence as they closed the shadow wall again.

"Raika?" Shane asked a minute later, his voice low, careful.

"Yes?" I rasped. Even speaking hurt my throat.

"I'm sorry. If I had known he would hurt you instead, I—"

"It's okay, Shane," I told him as I sat up. I was relieved Conri hadn't hurt Shane, because that would have hurt me more than physical pain. "What now? You're buying time? You think in less than twenty-four hours, your friends will be here?"

"Don't worry," he said, his voice low. "I've got a plan."

26

SHANE

For the next day, I waited for a miracle.

Once, one of Conri's demons came to report that they saw my friends outside the barrier. One witch trying to break the barrier, one vampire, and a handful of werewolves.

Even if Thea, Almae, and other vampires were on their way, I wasn't sure they would arrive in time to help me. I needed them here *before* the full moon.

As time passed, my hope faded.

And my dreaded plan B seemed to be our only choice.

During the past day, Raika and I received little food and water, and we had even fewer bathroom breaks—escorted by the demons and Conri's shadow magic.

Of course, each time they took me out, I tried breaking away, but the magic was too strong for me, especially with the damn cuffs around my wrists. In the end, I always returned to my cell with a new bruise.

Raika became quieter and quieter. I thought the pain Conri had inflicted on her and the day she had spent in the witch's circle outside, added to the starvation and isolation, were getting to her.

I couldn't blame her.

After a year living a nightmare, when things finally started looking up, it all came crashing down again.

I hadn't told her about my plan B. I wasn't so sure about it myself, and I had no idea of the outcome yet, but it was our only chance.

I could feel it deep in my bones as the full moon approached. Each day, each hour, each minute, closer and closer, stronger and stronger.

Then finally, the time came.

The sun was almost done setting when Conri and his demons came for me.

"Are you ready?" Conri asked as his demons opened the classroom's door.

He promptly wrapped my arms in shadows and aided as his demons tied my arms with some kind of magical rope in front of me. Why not tie them behind my back? Not that I was complaining.

As if reading my thoughts, the devil said, "I'm assuming you'll need to use your hands."

The demons pushed me out of the classroom and I stumbled forward. I was going to go, but I wouldn't make this easy for them.

Until Conri turned to Raika's door. His demons opened it and dragged her out. She looked weak and dizzy on her feet, her long hair dull and dirty, her face pale and her cheeks hollow.

My heart tugged.

"What are you doing?" I asked as the demons tied her hands behind her back.

"She's my insurance that you'll behave," Conri said, a wicked grin on his face. I would claw that grin out of his head. That was a damn promise. "Let's go."

Raika and I were taken to the main square. Streetlamps illuminated the space and directly in front of one of the broken benches in the four corners. The bench was gone but in its place was a round black mark, which looked suspiciously like a small trap door.

I frowned. Engraved on it was the Nightshade pack's symbol, the silhouette of a wolf's head in a silver line. Curiosity fought with reason and I found myself trying to open the trap door. I wanted to see the crystal. Maybe I could even use it to defeat Conri.

But when the full moon rose, I wouldn't need anything.

I knelt down beside the mark and ran my finger over it.

There were five small, round indentations. I wondered ... I placed my fingers in each of the ridges. A quick sting pricked my fingers, and I flinched from surprise. A small drop of blood fell from each finger.

A hiss escaped the trap door as it swung open.

Inside, a red crystal the size of my closed fist floated in the air in the chamber's center.

I reached for it.

Arms hooked around my shoulders and pulled me back.

"Finally," Conri said as he knelt beside the trap door and grabbed the crystal with his hands. He cradled it like a baby, his eyes shining. He didn't look at me when he said, "Get the others."

The demons tugged at me and pushed me to another corner of the square. Raika grunted as demons did the same to her. Behind us, Conri followed, but slowly, his body entranced by the crystal in his hands.

The demons pushed me to the ground in front of the next black mark. My knees slammed into the concrete. Pain jolted through my legs, and I gritted my teeth.

"Do it," a demon said, kicking me in the back.

"Stop it!" Raika snapped at him. One of the demons turned to her and raised his hand.

"Stop," I told him. "I'll do it."

The demon lowered his hand.

I looked up at the dark sky. The full moon was almost in position. I need a few more minutes, then this would be over. I had to stall a couple more minutes.

Knowing I couldn't escape this one without consequences, I repeated the process. I placed my fingers in the holes and didn't flinch this time when the needles pricked my skin.

The trap door opened and this time, I didn't even reach for the crystal. I stood and stepped back as Conri rushed forward and grabbed the second crystal in his hands. He stared at both of them, practically salivating with joy.

What was his deal with the crystals?

"Next one," Conri said without taking his eyes off the crystals.

This time, I slowed my steps, giving the demons pushing me a harder time. Halfway toward the next mark, I felt it.

The deep pull inside me, the warmth in my bones, the magic spreading through my skin.

The curse acted.

I glanced at Raika as I began shifting. "Run. Hide."

Her eyes widened.

A second later, I lost all conscious thoughts.

My limbs extended, my height increased, my form changed.

The Shadow Wolf had arrived.

27

RAIKA

I watched in horror as Shane shifted, but not into his usual big black wolf.

This one was big, it was black ... but it was something else. He didn't fall onto all fours. No, Shane stood on his legs, two heads taller than before, his limbs longer, thicker, his hands turned into sharp claws, his body covered in black fur and swirls of shadows, and his face a wolf's—with a long snout and sharp teeth, his eyes bright red.

The shackles broke from around his wrists like an elastic band.

I took a step back as he growled at the demons around us.

At me.

He didn't recognize me. That was why he had told me to run, to hide.

Oh, by the moon.

Shane attacked the demons and chaos ensued. More demons ran into the main square, coming for Shane, but he ripped through them as if they were made of paper.

The demons guarding me forgot about me and stepped forward to face Shane.

I retreated a few steps.

This wasn't Shane. I knew he had killed before, I knew he would kill again, but this massacre—bodies piled on the ground and blood spilled everywhere—this wasn't Shane. It couldn't be.

Several feet to my left, Conri handed the crystals to Dixon, who put them in a velvet pouch and hid it inside his jacket. Dixon nodded at Conri and broke into a run.

No! He couldn't get away with the crystals. We needed those.

I turned to follow him, to stop him, but the damn rope around my arms and the shackles around my wrists made it hard to run.

Without thinking about it, I called out. "Shane! The crystals!" I pointed to Main Street, where Dixon ran farther and farther from us.

Shane lifted his head from the fight and stared at me with those big red eyes.

Shit, what had I done?

A cold shiver slid down my spine as he stalked toward me, his lips pulled back, growling.

I stepped back. "Shane," I called, my voice trembling. "It's me, Shane." I retreated, but his legs were too long for mine. In half a dozen of steps, he halted in front of me, his huge shadowy body looming over mine. My legs shook. "I'm your mate, remember?"

Shane leaned over me, he sniffed my head, my shoulder. He reached down with his claws and cradled my arms in them. He lowered his head toward my hands, his mouth opening.

"Shane, no—" The words died in my lips as he bit down on the ropes and shackles and set me free. The broken shackles clanked on the floor—one of the most beautiful sounds I had ever heard.

Shane lifted his head, his eyes on mine. He had recognized me. He knew who I was. He poked his snout at my cheek, then turned and set into a fast run.

He lunged at Conri, who shifted into his demon-wolf—a four-legged wolf, bigger than most, with yellow eyes, and the same shadow magic around his body as Shane's. If it wasn't the same, it was similar.

Conri met Shane half-jump and the two of them rolled to the side and grappled.

Remembering the crystals, I turned toward Main Street. Dixon had a huge lead, but if I shifted into my wolf…

Giddiness filled me as I imagined shifting into my wolf once again. It had been so freaking long. I closed my eyes and let it happen. I welcomed a little pain as my limbs shifted, my bones changed, and my wolf took over.

I fell on all fours, my clothes ripped on the ground, and jumped in delight. I looked down at my paws—my light gray fur was back. Joy filled me.

I set out on a run after Dixon.

Not twenty yards after I started to run, a powerful force rammed into my side and I rolled as if I had been hit by a car. I slammed into a house's fence and whimpered as I stood and glanced up.

Phell, in his demon form, ran at me.

I skidded to the side, dodging his strike. Phell sent a wave of shadows at me—demonic magic. I ran to the side, he sent another wave my way. I changed directions and he sent it again.

Panting—I wasn't used to running and fighting anymore —I paused for a second. I couldn't outrun his magic.

Unless …

Phell swiped his arms wide, sending another wave of shadows toward me, a bigger, wider one.

Instead of running, I focused on it. I imagined myself jumping over the wave, rolling under it, stepping through without a problem.

Like it had happened before, when Phell killed my mother, the shadows parted and rolled past me.

"How?" Phell growled, his voice deep, rough. "How are you doing that? You've done it before. I remember."

I had no idea how, and honestly, I didn't care, as long as I could use it to win this damn fight. I charged Phell. With a snarl, he sent shadow bolts at me. Swift in my wolf form, I dodged them.

I wondered …

Phell sent another wave of bolts toward me.

I stopped and focused on them. They rounded me and zoomed toward him. Phell gasped and jumped to the side, but I had caught him by surprise and he wasn't fast enough. A couple hit his chest and shoulder, and he stumbled to the street's hard pavement.

My chance.

I jumped, clamping my teeth around his neck. He grabbed for my head, but I sank my teeth deep and twisted. His neck snapped, his body turned heavy.

I dropped him and stepped back, shocked.

I had killed him.

I had killed someone.

Shaking from horror and disgust, I reminded myself Phell

had been a demon, an evil one, and he had killed my mother and so many other people. He deserved this.

I stared at where Dixon had gone, to the end of the street. By now, he was at the edge of the pack lands. But maybe I could still catch up. I couldn't let him take the crystals.

A roar echoed behind me and I looked back to the main square. Shane, in his new form, attacked the demons defending Conri, ripping them apart as if they were paper.

Despite his scary appearance, Shane fared well against the demons, but I knew Conri was playing with him, tiring him so he could take Shane down.

I knew I had no chance to catch Dixon, so I ran toward Shane, my paws pounding the pavement. New voices and sounds reached my ears and I halted and turned to the source.

I gasped as supernaturals came in my direction—vampires zoomed past me, wolf shifters ran toward the fighting, and three witches halted beside me.

"Hi, I'm Lavinia," said a pretty woman with red-tipped black hair. "You must be Raika." I nodded. "This is Thea." She gestured to a blonde witch, then she pointed to the older witch taking off her long, black jacket. "And this my aunt, Almae. We are Shane's friends. Sorry it took so long, but we're here to help."

I shifted back—it hurt more than I remembered. Or perhaps my body wasn't used to it anymore. "You were able to break the barrier?"

Almae placed her jacket around my shoulders, covering my naked body. "Something changed," she said.

I thanked her and put on the jacket.

"The barrier became weak all of a sudden," she continued.

The crystals. When Conri took the crystals, the barrier weakened.

"After that, it didn't take long for us to break through."

"How can we help?" Thea asked. She wore an elegant black gown, which reminded me of the Nightmist witches—always dressed up for a ball. She was beautiful and looked to be in her mid to late twenties.

"Hm." I glanced at the battle next to us. With our allies, the demons fell fast. "I think ... we should rescue my pack. Free them from the classrooms they are locked in." I pointed to the school building.

Thea and Almae nodded and started toward the school. With automatic movements, I followed them, but Lavinia put her hand on my shoulder. "Shane might not have told you about the curse, so I won't. I'll let him explain the details to you, but when he's like this, he's not himself. After the fight is over, if he attacks our own, we'll have to subdue him. I just wanted you to know. We won't hurt him, but we have to stop him."

I frowned. "He didn't attack me."

Her eyes rounded. "What?"

"Yeah. Before ... he killed some demons then he came at me. I thought he would hurt me too, but he didn't. He sniffed me then he freed me." I showed her my bare wrists—the red bruises were still there and probably would be for a long time.

"So, he recognized you? That's ... great!" She grabbed my hand. "Come. You should be near him, then. When he turns on us, you can intervene."

I let her pull me closer to the main square, though I had to confess, I wasn't eager to try and calm down a feral wolf right now, even if it was my mate.

Shane grabbed a short demon with both his hands, and with a roar that made the hair on my arms stand on end, he pulled the demon apart, snapping his head off as if it was a bottle cap.

My stomach turned and a sliver of fear swirled in my chest.

Lavinia and I approached fray, where Shane turned to Conri again. The devil tried taking off, but the wolf shifters formed a blockade in front of him. Conri had been trying to get away, but no one was letting him.

A vampire with brown hair stepped closer to them. "No one interferes," he said. "This is Shane's kill."

"What? You're not going to help Shane?" I asked Lavinia, worried.

"Killian knows Shane would have wanted to do this himself. It's the only way for him to be alpha again."

"I ..." Honestly, I didn't know anymore. It had been that way before, but when a half-demon, half-wolf became alpha, all of the rules seemed to change.

The remaining wolf shifters killed the last of the demons, then formed a wide circle around Shane and Conri.

Conri snarled at Shane and conjured his magic. Shadows covered the ground around Shane, like dense fog. With a snarl, Shane charged Conri. Conri met him halfway in a wide jump. The two clashed hard. Conri went for Shane's throat, but Shane swiped his big claws down and scratched Conri's snout, pushing him away.

Conri fell on all four, but didn't retreat. He advanced again, trying to bite Shane, and Shane kept dodging the strikes and landing ones of his own.

Two strange wolves—one standing on two legs covered in

shadows, and the other a half-demon—fighting for my pack. You didn't see that every day.

Conri retreated as far as he could from Shane and turned, his eyes toward the full moon. The shadows on the ground rose, enveloping Shane.

I gasped and surged forward. Lavinia held my arm. "Don't."

"I can't just stand here and watch. Someone needs to help him." But as I said the words, I knew I couldn't. Lavinia was right. If I interfered now, Shane would forfeit the fight, and Conri would continue being alpha.

I couldn't allow that.

I swallowed my fear, pressed a hand to my stomach, and stayed put.

With a howl, Shane broke through the shadows, but not entirely. A bigger cloud of shadows swirled around him, weaving around his body, as if obeying his command.

Conri peeled his lips back in a snarl and covered his body in shadows as he lunged for Shane.

Movement and sounds coming from behind us caught my attention and I turned—I gasped as my pack clambered out of the school for the first time in a year! Tears filled my eyes. They all approached us, forming a wide arc around the improvised fighting circle. Among them, I saw Dom with a hand around Lucille's waist, helping her stand. She had a bruise on her cheek and neck, but nothing too bad.

Roman was right behind them, along with Jay, and Vianna and the pups. Serge kept his distance with two other older wolves.

Rue and Tyren accompanied Minsi as she ran for me, her eyes huge, her hands trembling. Minsi crashed into me and wrapped her arms around me. I embraced her tight. Rue stopped by my right and patted my shoulder.

To my left, Tyren frowned and watched the fight. "What's going on?"

Shit. "The tall one? That's Shane."

"What?" Tyren asked, his voice low, incredulous.

Shane grabbed Conri with both his claws and moved his big head toward Conri's throat, but the devil slinked away like a slippery eel.

Using his demon magic, Conri sent a wave of shadows toward Shane. But in this form, the shadows were Shane's friend. He stood tall and took the brunt of the wave—and from the deep breath he took, I could say he even absorbed some of it.

Conri continued sending hits at Shane—bolts, shards, anything he could think of—but Shane paused slightly each time one of the strikes hit him.

Always cheating, Conri turned and pushed through the crowd. The vampires around the ring didn't miss a beat. They pushed Conri back to the fight.

Without a choice, Conri turned back to Shane.

Suddenly, the shadows on the ground grew and formed a giant shadow wall around the ring. Before it closed, tendrils of shadow reached toward me. I stepped back and pushed Minsi to Rue. I fought the shadows, but they wrapped around my arms and legs and pulled at me. Tyren and Lavinia tried holding on to me but there was no use. The shadows swallowed me.

Three seconds of pure darkness, in which panic bloomed in my chest, but then it retreated.

I inhaled a sharp breath.

I was in the shadow ring with Shane and Conri.

Conri snarled at me as if poised to attack. Adrenaline and rage surged within me. I took off the jacket Almae gave me and shifted into my wolf, ready to attack him instead.

My mistake.

The moment I shifted, I heard someone else's voice in my mind.

Stop, Conri commanded.

My muscles froze. I could barely widen my eyes as realization hit me.

Conri was the alpha. I had never forgotten that, even though I had wanted to, but I had forgotten how the alpha could command his wolves—Conri rarely used that on me—and how he could communicate through a mind link when shifted.

That I had little experience with.

Shit.

But ... what about Shane? I had seen Conri's command working on Shane before, long ago, but it wasn't working now? Not while he was this monstrous shadow wolf?

Hesitating, Shane glanced from Conri to me and back to Conri. He let out a short snarl and charged Conri.

Kill him, Conri said in my mind.

A command.

My blood chilled as I felt the magic of the words surging, acting. My muscles moved and I turned to Shane.

Bastard, I said.

Conri laughed. *This will be fun.*

Conri didn't move as Shane ran at him because he knew he didn't have to. I rammed into Shane's side. He hadn't expected my strike and easily lost his balance. We tumbled to the ground, but he quickly shot up and bared his teeth at me.

Fear and despair gripped my chest, but I couldn't stop it. I wasn't in control of my body. I ran at him again, teeth snapping.

Stop this, I called to Conri.

The devil just laughed, the sound ringing in my head.

Making me sick.

My eyes welled with tears as I jumped at Shane again. I wasn't sure what was going on through his mind. If he still recognized me, if he thought I was a nuisance ... but he didn't stop me. He blocked my advances, he pushed me away, but he didn't strike me as hard as he could.

He didn't want to hurt me.

And I couldn't *not* hurt him.

Shane, I whispered, trying to reach his own mind. If you're listening, I can't control myself. You have to stop me.

There was no acknowledgment in his dark face, in his red eyes.

Even though he deflected each of my hits, I kept on going after him time and time again, tirelessly, stubbornly.

Finish him! Conri shouted in my mind.

I winced at the command.

But I couldn't help myself.

I aimed right and jumped, my mouth open so I could close it around Shane's neck.

Shane's arm swiped up and slapped as if I was a fly hovering around his head. I went flying through the air, then skidded across the ground, my body screaming at me as pain assaulted every inch of me.

Too tired and hurt, I lost the grip on my wolf and shifted back into my human form.

Shane loomed over me, his enraged eyes fixed on me, his claws turned to me, his fangs bared, rabid drool gathered at the corners of his mouth.

This was it.

My mate would kill me.

I just hoped this didn't kill him later.

"It's okay," I whispered before closing my eyes.

A moment later, Shane's snout pressed against my cheek. I opened my eyes wide, but didn't dare to move.

In a flash, Shane spun and charged Conri.

I stared, in shock.

Conri was probably yelling at me to kill Shane, but in my human form, I couldn't hear the mental link. Like this, I didn't feel the urge anymore.

I frowned, but didn't have time to think about it. I watched as Shane knocked Conri off his feet. The two of them tumbled to the hard ground and rolled around each other, while claws swiped and teeth snapped.

Confused if I should shift back and risk having Conri in my mind again, I kept my eyes peeled, looking for an opening regardless. If one presented itself, I would act. If I was fast enough, Conri's command wouldn't get to me in time.

But the two didn't stop moving.

I approached them and a moment later, they rolled over a flowerbed and its low metal fence. Conri whined and the two of them separated. They stood up, Shane on two legs, Conri on four, and faced each other again.

Shadows surged from beside Conri and advanced through the ring. Shane stepped right over it, as if it were smoke and it barely tickled his nose. He lunged at Conri as I braced myself for the wave as it quickly came at me and I had nowhere to go.

On instinct, I raised my hands like I had done before and the shadows faded into the air before connecting with me.

What?

I didn't waste time pondering about that. I ran toward Shane and Conri, who were at it again. Both of them tangled together, trying to hit and bite the other.

Quick as a snake, Conri bit down around Shane's shoulder. Shane howled in pain.

Oh, no. I shifted into my wolf, jumped on Conri's back, and closed my teeth around his side.

With a yelp, Conri let go of Shane and swiped at me, his shadows helping his action and giving him strength. I skidded across the pavement and hit my side on something hard. Pain laced my muscles.

Shane roared and charged Conri again. With renewed energy, Shane got the devil down, but as he straddled Conri, the devil bit his shoulder again. Shane howled but didn't let go. He swiped at Conri, making him lose his grip.

Then he closed his mouth around Conri's neck.

The cracking sound echoed through the ring.

I stared as Shane dropped Conri, and the devil's body slumped to the ground.

Conri was dead.

Relief filled me. I almost felt bad for rejoicing in someone's death, but I couldn't help it. Conri had ruined our lives and kept us as slaves for so long. There wasn't one ounce of sympathy or pity inside me, not for him.

Blood dripping from his mouth, Shane rose to his feet and turned to me. He snarled, showing off his sharp teeth.

I shifted back into my human form and raised both hands. "It's okay," I said in a soft voice. "We won. You're okay now. I'm okay now."

Shane stared at me, like a predator preparing to attack his prey, and I suddenly thought the moment we shared before had been a fluke. He had recognized me, but it had been a fluke. He didn't recognize me now.

Turning his face to the dark sky, he howled.

Then he charged at me.

My stomach tightened as an ounce of fear spread through me. I pushed it back, though. I stood my ground and faced him head-on. If he hurt me, if he killed ... then it was meant to be.

Shane skidded to a stop a foot from me. He lowered his big head to mine and wrapped his big furry arms around me. I was still unsure if he was about to bite me or if this was an awkward embrace ...

Before I could find out, he yelped and slipped to the ground.

"Shane." I went down with him, trying to hold on to such huge wolf as he passed out in my arms. I knelt beside him as his body shimmered and changed back into his human form. A sob of relief lodged in my throat. He was back! But my relief was short-lived as I saw the deep wound in his shoulder.

I opened my mouth to shout for help, but saw the shadow wall still in place. Conri had died but his demon magic was still active.

I frowned. I didn't think, I just did it. For Shane's sake. I closed my eyes and focused on the shadows. I reached for them in my mind, I caressed them with my touch, and they wrapped around me like a lost lover. I gasped, but did my best to hold on to that fragile connection. I closed my fists, imagining them coming undone.

And then they did.

The shadow walls melted into the ground as if they had never existed in the first place.

I stared, shocked and scared.

But I forgot all about it as everyone ran toward Shane and me.

"He needs a healer!" I yelled.

Several people came forward. Killian covered Shane's lower body with a blanket, Lavinia stood by my side and put a jacket back around my shoulders, the other two witches crouched beside Shane, and Jay, our healer, came closer, his hands trembling.

"I c-can help," he said, sounding a lot braver than I knew he was.

"We've got this," Thea said as she spread her hands over Shane's body. Almae did the same. A blue shine came from their palms, and slowly, Shane's wound mended. It didn't disappear, but it stopped bleeding and it closed well enough. She smiled at me. "He'll be all right."

"Thank you," I whispered.

I looked around me. Minsi was to my right with Rue and Tyren. Lucille and Dom were beside them, and the rest of our small pack behind them. To my other side, I saw Ironfang wolves, and directly in front of me were Shane's friends.

They had come to help us and now we were free.

I looked up at the night sky and inhaled deeply. Emotion filled my chest and my eyes brimmed with tears.

We were finally free.

There were many things to do, many things to figure out, many things to discuss and decide, but those could wait. Right now, right here, we were all right.

And somehow, we would make it last.

28

RAIKA

"Why are you doing this?" Roman asked as he walked beside me.

Though he had been free again for two days, Roman had promptly fallen into his old habit of checking in on me several times a day. Right now, he walked with me from my house, down Main Street, toward the town's center.

The sun was descending, bathing the town with an orangish golden light. If I squinted, I could pretend everything was okay. That everyone hadn't gone through a major trauma and it would take time for them—us—to heal.

"I have to ask him a few things," I told him and it wasn't a lie.

"He was always a jerk to you," Roman reminded me. "One of your bullies."

I winced. It had seemed that way to me too until I learned the truth a few days ago. But no one else knew.

"He's still our alpha," was all I said.

"You're moving from his house today, right?"

I shook my head. "Tomorrow. I can't leave Minsi alone

with Tyren, even if it's just for one night." Not that I didn't trust Tyren, but he was a teenager. I couldn't leave his anxiety and panic-prone sister in his care.

Roman nodded. He had helped move most of my things from Shane's house to mine earlier this morning when Minsi was with Rue.

I hadn't been there in a year. There had been no reason for me to go back, but now that the pack was free and Shane was back, it was time for me to live on my own.

It had been odd stepping into my house after so long. That was the place where my mother had died during the attack while trying to fight off Phell. Looking back, now I could see he hadn't tried hurting me. He wanted to take me to Conri unharmed, but my mother wouldn't let him. She fought with him.

And she lost.

I frowned. Had she known Conri wouldn't hurt me? Had she known why Conri wouldn't hurt me?

I glanced at my hands and remembered the shadows and how I had been able to part them, to control them. Until a handful of days ago, I had no idea. Was that related to why Conri had kept me alive?

Now I would never know.

Honestly, I didn't care. No one had seen it. I could pretend nothing had happened. I had never touched and controlled the shadows. I had never felt them like an extension of myself.

There. Erased from my mind.

"Everything all right?" Roman asked.

I didn't answer him right away. Instead, I looked ahead at the square as it came into view, and the wolves walking around, cleaning up the mess. In the distance, Vianna guided the kids inside the library.

Two days ago, we had defeated Conri and reclaimed our pack. The town was alive again and it warmed my heart.

"Yes," I whispered.

Most of our allies had left. Killian, Lavinia, and a handful of Killian's vampires stayed to help us clean up and rebuild. The Ironfang had also left after reminding Shane they had come when called and now Shane owed them one.

Our pack moved out of the school and into houses along the main street. Some were lucky to go back to their old houses, but some had lost their homes to the fire, so they took new-to-them houses.

Lucille had invited me to move in with her to her family's house, which was one of the biggest in town. I felt bad for her, but didn't think it was a good idea. She might have changed, but I was still wary around her. What if now that we were free, she decided to bully the omega again?

No, thank you.

Dom, though, was more than glad to move in with her.

Right now, I was still in the alpha's house with Minsi and Tyren. Despite his usual moodiness, Tyren seemed happy to be back, and tomorrow night, when Shane returned and I moved out, he and Minsi would be even happier.

We turned around the main square and I reached the town hall's front steps.

Roman caught my arm. "You don't need to talk to him."

I offered him a gentle smile. "It's okay, Roman. He can't hurt me." Roman had no idea how true those words were and why.

Maybe one day he would.

He crossed his arms and huffed, and I stepped into town hall by myself.

I had been here a couple of times in the past two days, but if Roman saw, he perhaps thought I was coming to talk to Lavinia or Killian, or one of the eldest wolves in the pack, who all claimed the council room as their own.

I sighed, remembering the amount of work we still had in front of us. Shane was keeping a list of things we should address soon: see who was left of the council, assign new posts, get the school up and running, create new security, start training again.

We were still missing two crystals. Dixon had gotten away with them, and the witches hadn't been able to recreate the barrier without them. Because of that, the weather was creeping in, and it was getting chilly. It was May, so at least we were heading into summer, but still, it would never be as warm and pleasant as it was when the barrier was up.

And we weren't protected. Anyone could come and go.

Anyone could attack us.

Besides everything he had to do for the town, Shane also wanted to come up with a plan to find and retrieve the crystals.

I was up for that, as we really needed the crystals back if we wanted our lives to be like they were before, but at the moment, I was so tired of fighting and fearing and crying, I needed a break.

We all did.

I walked down the stairs until I reached the prison. With the keys hanging beside the door, I unlocked it and walked in the cells' corridor.

Shane was in the last one, leaning on the metal bars, his eyes on me. I didn't bother locking the door behind me. I wouldn't be here for long and I trusted Shane to control his wolf long enough for me to run, if it came to that.

I walked toward him, mildly disappointed that since the attack, he had been wearing t-shirts along with his jeans. And shoes! My cheeks heated up thinking of the times he stalked to me wearing nothing but his pants.

I averted my gaze.

"What are you doing here?" Shane asked, his voice serious.

I shrugged as I approached his cell. "I guess I wanted to see how you are."

He frowned. "You came this morning. And yesterday afternoon. And yesterday morning. You know how I am."

I put my hands on my waist. "Are you complaining? Do you want me to leave?"

One corner of his lips curled up. "You know I don't." He grew serious again. "But sunset is a little over an hour away. I don't want you near here when the sun goes down."

I nodded.

For the last two days, Shane had asked to be kept in the cells, which had been reinforced by Thea and Almae before they left. Even so, he had set a curfew. Once the sun was down, everyone should stay inside their homes, and if he managed to escape, they were supposed to hide. If he found us, we were allowed to use anything to stop him from hurting us.

For the last two nights, everyone obeyed his order but me. I had joined Killian, Lavinia, and the other vampires in guarding the town hall. I wanted to be here in case he escaped. He had recognized me before; he could recognize me again.

I actually asked him about it yesterday, and he said he

didn't remember anything. While in his Shadow Wolf, he was out of it.

Even from inside his cell, Shane had shouted orders left and right, telling us what to do and how to fix everything. I knew staying locked down here while we worked relentlessly was killing him, so I didn't argue.

But tonight would be the last of the full moon cycle, and tomorrow the curfew would be lifted and Shane would be out of here. He would be able to run around with the rest of us, working all day and night to create a semblance of normalcy in our pack.

"Don't worry about that." I picked up the metal stool I had brought in yesterday and placed it right in front of his cell. I sat down. "Shane, I have a request."

He crouched beside me, the metal bars in between us. "What is it?"

"Tell me about the curse." I knew this could wait, but I also knew that if given the chance, he would run from the question. While in here, he had nowhere to go.

Shane groaned. "Raika ..."

"I want to know. As your mate, I have a right to know." I hated playing the mate card, but it was true. He shouldn't hide anything from me.

Even if I was hiding my unknown power over the shadows from him.

He let out a sigh. "After they took me away, the Nightmist witches cursed me. They used blood magic to make me what they called a Shadow Wolf during the full moon. Every full moon, I lose control. The Shadow Wolf overtakes me and I have no idea what I'm doing. I've been told I attack everyone, any of my friends ... but you. Though, we can't count on that. We don't know why, if it's because you're my mate, or something else. I would rather not risk it again."

"How can we break it?"

"A Nightmist witch needs to do another spell, using blood magic, to undo it. It's supposed to be simple. But the problem is finding a willing Nightmist witch."

"We'll find one. While we look for the crystals, we can also look for the witches. "

"There aren't many of them left now, and I bet they are all hiding."

"It doesn't matter. We'll find them." I was sure we would. I didn't know how or when, but we certainly would.

"There's more," he said, his voice low.

My back straightened. "What is it?"

"This curse … it's supposed to take over. Not just during the full moon. The longer the curse afflicts me, the worse it'll be. Soon, I won't shift into the Shadow Wolf just during the full moon. It'll start getting longer and longer, and then it'll happen when I'm angry … until I lose myself to the curse completely."

I gasped. "You're saying, if we don't break the curse soon, you'll become the Shadow Wolf."

He nodded.

I reached for him through the bars. His hand met mine halfway and he entwined his fingers with mine.

"I don't want to hurt you," he said. "I don't want to hurt anyone."

"That won't happen. We'll break this curse before that."

"We need to break the curse, to find the crystals, rebuild the town, make sure everything is okay." He let out a long sigh. "We have lots to do."

I nodded. "That we do."

"And we'll do everything together. I'm not leaving you alone ever again."

"You better not." I reached in with my other arm and soft-punched him in the ribs.

He groaned, pretending to be hurt. Then Shane brought our hands up and kissed the top of mine, his lips soft and warm on my skin. "That's a promise."

EPILOGUE
PAIMON

THE DEMON DIXON KNELT BEFORE ME AND LIFTED HIS HANDS, offering me two red crystals. "For you, my prince."

A grin spread over my lips and I reached for the crystals. Instantly, their magic tickled me and I inhaled deeply, already energized. When I fueled the magic within, when I used it, I would be stronger …

I stared at the crystals in my hands.

When the king of the underworld fell and his children took over a few years ago, I had to run. The moment King Brikan died, I felt my magic fading, but when I fled the underworld with the other princes, the magic left my veins almost altogether. I survived on sacrifices and magical objects I found and could absorb magic from. I wasn't sure that was happening to the other princes, but I didn't care.

What I cared about was my energy, my magic. I would be strong again, stronger than before. And when I did, I would take the underworld back.

I would be the new king of the underworld, and even the other princes would bow to me.

And these crystals were the first step.

"What about Conri?" I asked.

Dixon stared at my feet as he answered, "He stayed back, my prince. From the report I received, he perished fighting the previous alpha heir."

I frowned.

From the moment I found the half-wolf, half-demon lost and alone, took him in, and gave him purpose, Conri had been a good lackey. Because I was too weak, when I made the deal with the Nightmist witches to attack the Nightshade pack, I had sent him in my place. He was supposed to find the crystals and bring them to me, even if that took centuries.

It had taken only a year to find them all, even if I only had two now. The other two crystals would be mine soon. At least now the barrier protecting the pack lands was gone.

It would be easy to attack.

To take.

To kill.

"What about Raika?" I asked. "Did Conri treat her well? Was she hurt during the fight?"

"Conri never hurt her permanently, and she wasn't hurt during the fight."

A wave of rage swept through me. Conri didn't hurt her *permanently*? What in the underworld did that mean? That he had hurt her? I had told him to treat her well, to make sure she was okay and never in any pain. To shower her with all she needed.

If that demon was still alive, I would kill him myself.

I gripped the crystals tight as a plan formed in my mind. "I think it's time I paid my daughter a visit."

THANK you for reading *The Night Calling*! If you liked it, don't forget to pre-order book 2, *The Night Burning*: https://geni.us/TNBurning-Am

If you would like to read how everything changed for Shane and Raika (aka: Minsi's 10th birthday party, how they found out about the mating bond, and Conri's attack), then enter this link on your browser: https://dl.bookfunnel.com/xxtalusxkv

Haven't you read Killian's and Lavinia's story yet? Then download *The Darkest Vampire* at https://geni.us/TDVampire-Am and start their trilogy now! That's where Shane is first introduced in the story ;)

Also, join my Facebook group (https://www.facebook.-com/groups/JulianasClub) to get another exclusive book, *The Light Witch*. The main characters in this book, Evelyn and Ash, will show up on book 2 of Shane+Raika's series!

THANK YOU

Thank you for reading *The Night Calling*!

Reviews are very important for authors. If you liked my book, please consider leaving a review on your favorite online retailer and/or on Goodreads and/or Bookbub, please!

Did you like this book? You can check out other books of mine:

The Darkest Vampire (Rite World: Vampire Wars book 1): a witch releases a dark vampire from a curse, and becomes inadvertently bonded to him.

The Midnight Test (Rite World: Lightgrove Witches book 1): a clueless witch is invited to join a powerful coven—but only if she aces a difficult test.

The Demon Kiss (Rite World: Blackthorn Hunters Academy book 1): a fast-paced story about a young woman who finds out she's a demon hunter, and the half-demon intent on protecting her against all evil.

The Vampire Heir (Rite World 1: Rite of the Vampire): a

dark and mysterious paranormal romance about a vampire and a young woman with a secret.

The Warlock Lord (Rite World 4: Rite of the Warlock): a thrilling and kick-ass paranormal romance about a werewolf and warlock.

The Wolf Forsaken (Rite World 7: Rite of the Wolf): a heat-wrenching tale about a lost wolf shifter and a fae princess on the run.

Heart Seeker (The Fire Heart Chronicles book 1): an urban fantasy series about a young woman who finds herself at the center of a mysterious supernatural world.

Destiny Gift (The Everlast Series book 1): a post-apocalyptic urban fantasy series about a young woman with a special power that can save the world.

ABOUT THE AUTHOR

While USA Today Bestselling Author Juliana Haygert dreams of being Wonder Woman, Buffy, or a blood elf shadow priest, she settles for the less exciting—but equally gratifying—life as a wife, a mother, and an author. She resides in North Carolina and spends her days writing about kick-ass heroines and the heroes who drive them crazy.

Subscribe to her mailing list to receive emails of announcement, events, and other fun stuff related to her writing and her books: www.bit.ly/JuHNL

For more information:
www.julianahaygert.com

facebook.com/julianahaygert

twitter.com/julianahaygert

instagram.com/juliana.haygert

goodreads.com/juliana_haygert

pinterest.com/julianahaygert

bookbub.com/authors/juliana-haygert

youtube.com/julianahaygert

tiktok.com/@julianahaygert

ALSO BY JULIANA HAYGERT

To find links and more info, go to:

www.julianahaygert.com/books/

Shorts

Into the Darkest Fire

Standalones

Daughter of Darkness

Rite World: Night Wolves

The Night Calling (Book 1)

The Night Burning (Book 2)

The Night Hunting (Book 3)

The Night Rising (Book 4)

Rite World: Vampire Wars

The Darkest Vampire (Book 1)

The Darkest Witch (Book 2)

The Darkest Magic (Book 3)

Rite World: Lightgrove Witches

The Midnight Test (Book 1)

The Midnight Spell (Book 2)

The Midnight Flame (Book 3)

Earth Shaker (Book 2.5)

Sorrow Bringer (Book 3)

Soul Wanderer (Book 4)

Fate Summoner (Book 5)

War Maiden (Book 6)

The Everlast Series

Destiny Gift (Book 1)

Soul Oath (Book 2)

Cup of Life (Book 3)

Everlasting Circle (Book 4)

Willow Harbor Series

Hunter's Revenge (Book 3)

Siren's Song (Book 5)

Breaking Series

Breaking Free (Book 1)

Breaking Away (Book 2)

Breaking Through (Book 3)

Breaking Down (Book 4)

www.ingramcontent.com/pod-product-compliance
Lightning Source LLC
Chambersburg PA
CBHW060928190726

48286CB00002B/676